# L. RON HUBBARD

# All Frontiers Are Jealous

GALAXY PRESS

Published by
Galaxy Press, LLC
7051 Hollywood Boulevard, Suite 200
Hollywood, CA 90028

Printed in the United States of America.

ISBN-10 1-59212-254-X
ISBN-13 978-1-59212-254-7

Library of Congress Control Number: 2007903546

# Contents

# Stories from Pulp Fiction's Golden Age

A ND it *was* a golden age.

The 1930s and 1940s were a vibrant, seminal time for a gigantic audience of eager readers, probably the largest per capita audience of readers in American history. The magazine racks were chock-full of publications with ragged trims, garish cover art, cheap brown pulp paper, low cover prices—and the most excitement you could hold in your hands.

"Pulp" magazines, named for their rough-cut, pulpwood paper, were a vehicle for more amazing tales than Scheherazade could have told in a million and one nights. Set apart from higher-class "slick" magazines, printed on fancy glossy paper with quality artwork and superior production values, the pulps were for the "rest of us," adventure story after adventure story for people who liked to *read*. Pulp fiction authors were no-holds-barred entertainers—real storytellers. They were more interested in a thrilling plot twist, a horrific villain or a white-knuckle adventure than they were in lavish prose or convoluted metaphors.

The sheer volume of tales released during this wondrous golden age remains unmatched in any other period of literary history—hundreds of thousands of published stories in over nine hundred different magazines. Some titles lasted only an issue or two; many magazines succumbed to paper shortages during World War II, while others endured for decades yet. Pulp fiction remains as a treasure trove of stories you can read, stories you can love, stories you can remember. The stories were driven by plot and character, with grand heroes, terrible villains, beautiful damsels (often in distress), diabolical plots, amazing places, breathless romances. The readers wanted to be taken beyond the mundane, to live adventures far removed from their ordinary lives—and the pulps rarely failed to deliver.

In that regard, pulp fiction stands in the tradition of all memorable literature. For as history has shown, good stories are much more than fancy prose. William Shakespeare, Charles Dickens, Jules Verne, Alexandre Dumas—many of the greatest literary figures wrote their fiction for the readers, not simply literary colleagues and academic admirers. And writers for pulp magazines were no exception. These publications reached an audience that dwarfed the circulations of today's short story magazines. Issues of the pulps were scooped up and read by over thirty million avid readers each month.

Because pulp fiction writers were often paid no more than a cent a word, they had to become prolific or starve. They also had to write aggressively. As Richard Kyle, publisher and editor of *Argosy*, the first and most long-lived of the pulps, so pointedly explained: "The pulp magazine writers, the best of them, worked for markets that did not write for critics or attempt to satisfy timid advertisers. Not having to answer to anyone other than their readers, they wrote about human beings on the edges of the unknown, in those new lands the future would explore. They wrote for what we would become, not for what we had already been."

Some of the more lasting names that graced the pulps include H. P. Lovecraft, Edgar Rice Burroughs, Robert E. Howard, Max Brand, Louis L'Amour, Elmore Leonard, Dashiell Hammett, Raymond Chandler, Erle Stanley Gardner, John D. MacDonald, Ray Bradbury, Isaac Asimov, Robert Heinlein—and, of course, L. Ron Hubbard.

In a word, he was among the most prolific and popular writers of the era. He was also the most enduring—hence this series—and certainly among the most legendary. It all began only months after he first tried his hand at fiction, with L. Ron Hubbard tales appearing in *Thrilling Adventures, Argosy, Five-Novels Monthly, Detective Fiction Weekly, Top-Notch, Texas Ranger, War Birds, Western Stories,* even *Romantic Range.* He could write on any subject, in any genre, from jungle explorers to deep-sea divers, from G-men and gangsters, cowboys and flying aces to mountain climbers, hard-boiled detectives and spies. But he really began to shine when he turned his talent to science fiction and fantasy of which he authored nearly fifty novels or novelettes to forever change the shape of those genres.

Following in the tradition of such famed authors as Herman Melville, Mark Twain, Jack London and Ernest Hemingway, Ron Hubbard actually lived adventures that his own characters would have admired—as an ethnologist among primitive tribes, as prospector and engineer in hostile climes, as a captain of vessels on four oceans. He even wrote a series of articles for *Argosy,* called "Hell Job," in which he lived and told of the most dangerous professions a man could put his hand to.

Finally, and just for good measure, he was also an accomplished photographer, artist, filmmaker, musician and educator. But he was first and foremost a *writer,* and that's the L. Ron Hubbard we come to know through the pages of this volume.

This library of Stories from the Golden Age presents the best of L. Ron Hubbard's fiction from the heyday of storytelling, the Golden Age of the pulp magazines. In these eighty volumes, readers are treated to a full banquet of 153 stories, a kaleidoscope of tales representing every imaginable genre: science fiction, fantasy, western, mystery, thriller, horror, even romance—action of all kinds and in all places.

Because the pulps themselves were printed on such inexpensive paper with high acid content, issues were not meant to endure. As the years go by, the original issues of every pulp from *Argosy* through *Zeppelin Stories* continue crumbling into brittle, brown dust. This library preserves the L. Ron Hubbard tales from that era, presented with a distinctive look that brings back the nostalgic flavor of those times.

L. Ron Hubbard's Stories from the Golden Age has something for every taste, every reader. These tales will return you to a time when fiction was good clean entertainment and the most fun a kid could have on a rainy afternoon or the best thing an adult could enjoy after a long day at work. Pick up a volume, and remember what reading is supposed to be all about. Remember curling up with a *great story*.

—Kevin J. Anderson

KEVIN J. ANDERSON *is the author of more than ninety critically acclaimed works of speculative fiction, including* The Saga of Seven Suns, *the continuation of the* Dune Chronicles *with Brian Herbert, and his* New York Times *bestselling novelization of L. Ron Hubbard's* Ai! Pedrito!

# All Frontiers Are Jealous

# Chapter One

A few months ago there appeared in the London *Times* a financial notice. The bankers saw nothing unusual about it. The public paid it little heed. Investors shied. A few brokers smiled. Only a few knew the undiluted hell which backed those dry, crisp lines.

SUDAN RAILWAY
TRIED AGAIN
Colonel Malone Asks Aid in
Long-Abandoned Project

*Mombasa, Kenya, EEA,* March 6 (RS)—Rumors of yet another effort to link the Uganda Railway with the Anglo-Egyptian Railroad were confirmed here by Colonel B. A. Malone, well-known promoter.

Investors will remember the disaster of former ventures when all attempts to survey the line failed.

Colonel Malone, according to his statement, will utilize a short franchise granted him to survey the line. He will attempt to float a loan on the London market.

The only memorandum made concerning this item was handed out to outer-office clerks and read, "No matter what price offered, we are not to be bothered with SR bonds."

However, down in Mombasa and shortly in Nairobi, Colonel Malone grew expansive and hopeful as always. Optimism sprouted from him like green bamboo shoots. He had won and lost half a dozen fortunes but no incident in his life had ever dimmed his winning, if gold-plated smile.

Railroads made money. Colonel Malone made railroads. He had shot his quota of lions at Tsavo. He had sunk his pick into the clay of Tanganyika. He could wave his hand at a map and truthfully say that the thing would be a blank if he hadn't helped matters with railroads.

And, that hot and depressing afternoon, when he alighted at Nairobi in company with a weather-beaten young giant, he ran true to form by saying:

"When I first saw this place, Dan, it was ten mud huts and a sheet-iron shed. Look at it now! Modern. Electric lights! Streets. A post office! We did that with the Uganda Railway. She's a beaut, isn't she, what?"

Dan Courtney glanced at the stubby, woodburning engine which was panting wearily after its run. He listened for a moment to the yapping roar of the natives in third class.

"Yeah," said Dan Courtney, "she's a beaut."

"And the first thing you know," said Colonel Malone, "the fetid green of jungle and the golden sands of desert will be caressed with the steel highway into the north. Think of it, Dan!"

"Yeah," said Dan. He raised his khaki sun hat and mopped at his brow and gazed longingly down the blazing street at a veranda which looked cool.

"In chains," whispered Malone, ecstatically. "Like a mighty

beast, the Dark Continent growls and snarls at us, but within the decade the last link between the Mediterranean and the Indian Ocean will be welded. Progress, Dan, what?"

"Yeah. But I'm not in the market for stock in it. Let's get us a drink of lemon pop or something."

Malone's smile grew sad. "You've no imagination, Dan. No imagination. But then . . . no American ever had an imagination. Leave that and empire to the British, what?"

"Lemonade," persisted the weathered giant. "I got to work the rest of the day."

"Look here," said Malone, "you're not getting cold feet, are you?"

Dan looked down at the heat waves which shivered off the concrete around his scorched boots and grinned.

"You're not going to back out, are you? Look here, Dan, you can't do that! Just because those damned Dinkas murdered Stephans and slaughtered Lawry's men. . . . You wouldn't let that stop *you*, would you, Dan?"

"Who said anything about quitting? A job is a job. I've got to stretch a line from Lake Salisbury and the Uganda to the Anglo-Egyptian at Sennar across the Sudan. I've got to review Lawry's work and confirm his passes and grades and take a blank out of the map in the Dinka country. For that I get three hundred bucks a month and five hundred in stock. It's a job. Let's find some lemonade."

They turned toward the street, starting to thrust their way through the press of natives about the station. But they did not get very far. Two white men of burly build stood in the way and seemed to have heard Dan's last remark. One was short and wide, the other was tall and wide. This last had a narrow head on which two very small, pointed ears were set. One of these ears was half gone. The smaller one's nose took up twice as much territory as it should have and his eyes took up only half their allotted space.

"If it ain't Malone," said the bigger man.

The colonel's pleasant expression hardened like concrete. "Hello, Gotch-ear. I see the local authorities are asleep as usual."

"He kids all the time just like that, Bart," said Gotch-ear to his short friend. "Did I hear Salisbury to Sennar, Malone?"

"That missing chunk don't seem to hurt your hearing any," growled the colonel.

"This tall boy making a safari up by Alak?" persisted Gotch-ear.

"I'll take a safari over your frame if you don't get out of my way," snapped the colonel.

"You wouldn't be thinking of tagging us, would you, big guy?"

"I pick clean trail when I travel, whatever-the-hell-your-name-is," said Dan.

"A Yank," said Gotch-ear. "Listen, big guy, keep your eye on your transit up north. I don't take nothin' from punks, see? And if this is one of your sneaks, Malone, we'll send you back your pal's head in a big wicker basket."

Gotch-ear and Bart moved off into the swarm of natives and were lost. Dan, with a singleness of purpose which was very characteristic of him, headed for the veranda and the cold drink.

"I fired him off the South African road," explained Malone. "He was stealing supplies and selling them. Wonder what the hell he's doing in Nairobi."

"From his looks, it isn't legal," said Dan. "He's jittery."

"Must be important. Gotch-ear's got a nose for money. Wonder why he made a point of heading you off."

"Jittery, that's all," said Dan. "Forget it. Northern Uganda is big enough for a dozen Gotch-ears."

"I wonder if he's being paid to block this road," puzzled Malone, trying to keep up with Dan's long stride and half running to do it in spite of the heat.

"Nuts," said Dan. "All you need is this survey, the franchise and the cash. You'll have the first two and you'll get the third, won't you?"

"The cash?" blinked Malone. "Oh . . . oh yes, of course. Sure I'll get it. I'll float a bond issue on the London market. Sure, that's easy. They'll snap up the SR paper like it was printed on platinum."

A tall and dignified native stepped out from the questionable shade of a warehouse and accosted Dan with great ceremony.

"You look well, *bwana*."

"Hello, Petey," said Dan. "Been having good luck?"

"No, *bwana*."

"Maybe I'll change it for you. Scout out and round up the boys you wired me you had. We scurry out of here this afternoon."

"Yes, *bwana*," said Petey, withdrawing with another bow.

Dan slid into a chair beside a veranda table, pulled off his helmet and fanned lazily at his moist face.

"As soon as I get the equipment together," said Dan, presently, "I'll take that train to the end of the line at Soroti. I want to be well into the country when the rains start."

"You bet you do," said Malone. "You've got eight months to run the line and that's not half enough time. My . . . er . . . ah . . . franchise runs out at that time, you know."

"The bonus of two grand still sticks?"

"Of course. Africa . . ."

Dan didn't listen to the colonel. His attention had been distracted by a very soft and lovely voice at the next table. He squared around slightly, and instantly the lazy boredom froze on his face.

He did not know the girl, but he knew he would very shortly. He had never seen his destiny so plain before him.

His blue gaze intently surveyed her as though he was topographing a range of hills.

She had a sun helmet on the back of her head and blond, damp curls were escaping from under the band. She had a very serious look on her face as well as three spots of lead smudge, deposited by a habit of biting worriedly at her pencil with small white teeth.

She wore a shooting jacket unbuttoned at the throat, a khaki walking skirt and a pair of battered sixteen-inch laced boots, one of which bobbed back and forth displaying a sole which looked too small to be believed.

She wrinkled up her pert nose, scowled dreadfully, gave her sun hat a bothered shove and, gnawing the pencil, looked abstractedly around.

Dan was too engrossed in a careful contouring of her head to whip his eyes away in time.

Their gaze met, grew warm, flared and Dan looked hastily away.

"The romance of Africa . . ." Colonel Malone was saying.

Dan thought that over and then took a sight across his glass at the girl again. She was still looking at him.

"Umm," said Dan, "you're right, Colonel. Dead right."

"Of course I'm right. She's a black-hearted beast, treacherous and unforgiving. . . ."

"What?" said Dan. "Oh . . . Africa. Yes, yes, indeed, Colonel."

"I'll show her she can't intimidate me. You just plow right through, Tuaregs or no Tuaregs. Take your sights, find the passes and we'll have a line running . . ."

Dan was listening to the girl's voice. She was talking to a man he had, for the first time, noticed. A beaten, gray-haired chap, with a glint of humor in his washed-out eyes, showed some of the girl's facial characteristics. A good-looking old chap, well dressed and capable. He'd seen Africa before.

She was saying, "Three tents, five canteens, six more loads of *posho,* shells for my ten-seventy-five by sixty-eight . . . Think we'll meet any elephants on Mount Alak?"

"It would look better," said the old man. "You're the judge, Barbara."

Dan blinked. Mount Alak was north of Lake Salisbury, beside his route.

Without thinking, he said, "Sure you'll see elephants up

there. But don't you think ten-seventy-five is a pretty tough baby for a girl? I'd suggest . . ."

Coolly, evidently ruffled by his allusion to her capabilities, Barbara took the pencil out of her mouth and said, "Perhaps you'd suggest an air rifle for elephants. I don't believe I've had the pleasure, sir."

Dan was very disconcerted. He should have known women were sensitive and that they despised men who told them they were not as good at man's games as men.

Unreasonably, Dan growled, "Nobody ever could tell a tenderfoot anything anyhow. Get your shoulder broke and see if I care. Come along, Colonel, I've got to get my outfit and find Petey."

He stamped down the steps and turned toward the depot and the colonel came up beside him, trotting to compensate the difference in leg length.

They had not gone ten steps before Dan thrust an elbow into the colonel's midriff, depriving him of a considerable quantity of breath.

When they reached the depot, the colonel huffed, "What was the idea? Trying to knock me out?"

"Did you see them?"

"See who?"

"That guy Gotch-ear and his pal Bart," said Dan. "If I ever saw a pair of vultures in my life, they're it."

"What about them?"

Dan looked sober. "They were across the street, standing in the shade looking up at the veranda."

"Watching us," said Malone.

"Nix," replied Dan. "They were keeping tabs on that girl and the old man."

"None of our business," said Malone with typical African fatalism.

"I guess not," said Dan. "There's Petey now with the boys."

# Chapter Two

THE slightly bored giant of Nairobi and the harassed surveyor of the mucky Sobat River bore little resemblance to each other. Minor things such as fever, big cats, flies, hunger, rain, thirst, weariness and mutinous porters had taken a fairly decent bit of sculptured humanity and, with these chisels of fate, had lopped off all excess fat and had, with lines of concern, added a new aspect to the face.

The rhino who was standing out of sight in a clump of brush had no chance to make a comparison. His eyesight was bad anyway and he failed to appreciate the way the Sudan was treating big Dan Courtney. He relied, that rhino, upon the scent the wind brought to him and from time to time he stamped and grumbled and thrust his horn this way and that to get a new whiff. It was taking him some little time to get really angry. Besides, it was hot. Soon he would get an idea that all was not well and, with astounding speed and terrific momentum, working up a few million foot-pounds of kinetic energy, he would charge to investigate.

On top of an anthill to the east sat a Dinka scout in an identical frame of mind. But he had a little more intelligence than the rhino and he did not have to charge to know that there in the marshes below was a white man evidently persistent in heading northward at any cost.

This Dinka scout was almost six feet tall. He was of a dark complexion but his features were not Negroid. He had thin lips which registered, at the moment, cruelty. His nose was thin and straight and his eyes were very clear. He carried a long iron spear and, for protection, his arms were cased in iron rings.

He knew, did this Dinka, that the last time the ignorant, bad-smelling, useless, braggadocio, ugly whites had tried to run a rail survey through here, not one single man had been left alive through courtesy of one *Bain*, the rainmaker, a man of great resource.

Oblivious of all this, Dan Courtney had eyes for a red and white pole which was balanced none too well between the curled fingers of a rodman.

The sight—God be praised—was over a hundred yards all in one piece. It was clean and no *panga* work had been necessary. It was nothing less than an omen of future good fortune. His bad breaks were at an end. Ahead the marshes might open up, this fifteen-foot grass might disappear, the ground might even become dry.

Good luck ahead, no less.

He had found the passes in sight of snowcapped mountains. He had shivered in thin blankets as he made up his notes and figured his shots. He had struggled through the torrents of rain, which snapped the spider webbing in his transit, and had carved a trail through jungle.

He had shot lions with one hand and worked his slipstick with the other. He had cursed the monkeys for tearing up his stakes, the elephants for trampling them down. He had figured bridges across flooding streams, cuts along precipices, fills over bogs, and grades down mountains. He had worked in the altitude of a mile down to two thousand feet and now, having struck the White Nile, he was wallowing through the mosquito-infested sudd.

Lost out of the map, he had left a trail of stakes and *panga*-slashed jungle stretching behind him for six hundred miles and more, and he still had four hundred to go.

But ahead of him lay flat, if marshy, land. He could ride his compass the rest of the way. No more wandering dazedly around peaks looking for a way through. No more lying awake three nights in a row, raving mad because he could not find an easy grade down.

Straight ahead, marking everything "fill." Straight ahead to Sennar.

He was five months on his way. He had three months to go. He was making a record for speed.

Only a dogged, stubborn will to do his job had kept him going. The survey had to go through. No heroics about it for Dan Courtney. He had tackled stuff almost as bad as this.

He waved his right hand, trying to get the rodman to straighten the red and white stick which stood with its metal point on a scrap of paper which marked a station. The colors shivered in the oven heat of the swamp. Steam made the image dim and hazed the lenses of the transit.

He barked a string of degrees, minutes and seconds at his partly educated recorder and the weary, half-naked half-caste scribbled them down in the book.

Dan mopped at his sweatband, turned his telescope and

took his back sight. The rodman there was very busy swatting mosquitoes, and the rod, which should have been stonily perpendicular, was weaving around like a semaphore signal.

Dan raised his right hand. Nothing happened—or, that is, the rod moved more restlessly than ever. Dan raised his left and right, but the rodman was apparently blind, suffering from Saint Vitus' dance.

Dan stood back and put his hands on his hips. He was weary and his temper was as ragged as his khaki shooting jacket. His mouth grew taut for an instant and then opened up with a bellow of rage which would have done credit to a crocodile bull.

"By the fifteen green-eyed, triple-tailed cats, what the hell do you think you're doing with that rod?"

The rodman stiffened. So did the hidden rhino.

Instantly the rhino conceived that this was a matter which needed much investigation. His thirty-horsepower, direct-drive engines grumbled within him. He picked up speed. He came into sight like a slow-motion picture of a sixteen-inch shell gathering momentum and bent on shattering itself against anything which got in its straight path.

"Rhino!" screamed the recorder and fled.

"Rhino!" squealed the gun boy, Lippy, heading for the nearest bush and taking Dan's Mauser with him.

The transit was glittering, the easiest target. The rhino picked that for its target and came on at a gallop, doubling, tripling in size.

Dan tried to scoop up his transit, slipped and fell sprawling. He hitched himself to one side.

*The transit was glittering, the easiest target. The rhino*
*picked that for its target and came on at a gallop,*
*doubling, tripling in size.*

The colossus loomed over him. The big, thundering feet stamped three feet away from his hand.

Dan, with a short prayer, closed his eyes tight and waited. But he allowed himself a promise that he would skin Lippy alive for deserting—if he, Dan, ever lived that long. The mortality of gun bearers is greatly exceeded by that of their *bwana*s.

There was a horrible, smashing clatter, a rending of wood and metal. There came a snort which made Dan's neckcloth quiver.

Dan opened one eye cautiously.

The rhino had demolished the transit, had charged ahead, had failed to recognize anything else to charge and was now wheeling clumsily like a ten-ton truck, looking around slightly mystified as to the disappearance of that glittering thing it had first sighted. It failed to realize that it had struck anything.

It muttered about it, tossed its head a few times threateningly for luck, glared all about and then stopped. Suddenly a tick dug a bit too deeply and the rhino managed to feel it through its armor plate. A rhino bird would take care of that. Besides, it was too hot out in the sun.

The nightmare beast lumbered back toward its thicket, everything forgotten.

But not forgiven.

Dan Courtney stood up and slabbed the mud from his chest and knees, swearing all the while in a horrible monotone. He inspected his transit and found it ruined. The levels were broken, the compass face was cracked, the telescope was bent into a graceful U.

The disaster was not quite fatal. Dan had the parts and pieces of three more transits in his baggage and, with a little whittling on the tripod and a few substitutions, he could make it right.

But that all took time and Dan had but very little time to spare. The surveying of four hundred miles in three months is the height of speed even in good country. It meant that he would have to average about four and a half miles per day, seven days a week. While he was only marking the way and proving that a road could go through, four and a half miles is a good trek.

While he was still swearing, Petey, his headman, came hurriedly back to him.

At first Dan thought Petey had heard the rhino charge, but then he saw that the headman bore a package under his arm and that three porters were following him with other packages.

Petey made a ceremony of everything. He was well educated for a native and this made him a little haughty with his fellows and, therefore, a good leader. But he was a pessimist from a long line of pessimists and, after the African fashion, he was extremely superstitious.

Petey overlooked the wrecked transit. He lined up his boys. He bowed to Dan and then extended a bundle.

"One half mile ahead," said Petey with dignity, "I was busy chaining. I came upon a game trail which runs in our direction through the marsh. Just before I had said to—"

"Get on with it," said Dan. "What's this? Why did you knock off work?"

With greater dignity than ever, Petey said, "I had just said to Jujo, 'I think it is time we struck the Dinka route.' And then I chanced to glance down and I observed a footprint."

"Yes, yes, there's only a few hundred thousand Dinkas ahead. What about it?"

"This footprint," said Petey, severely, "was made by a small boot worn by a person of light weight who was very weary. It was three days old. It had part of the heel worn down. The person was white and wore a khaki shooting jacket."

"What the hell are you talking about? There's no white person within two hundred miles of here. Good God, Petey, I haven't got time to listen to your imagination work. Get back to work!"

"*Bwana,*" said Petey, more regal than ever, "observe this bundle."

Dan did so. He opened it up and saw, much to his dismay and surprise, a gold compact, two small handkerchiefs and a pair of eyebrow tweezers.

"That fell from a pocket which was ripped on a bush. This white person," said Petey, satisfied of Dan's interest now, "was running and very tired."

"But holy smoke!" cried Dan. "A compact on the upper reaches of the Nile? Petey, am I dreaming? Is this Broadway and Forty-second or is this White Nile and Sobat? Am I nuts? Petey. Look at me. Are we or are we not in the middle of Africa?"

"Africa, *bwana.*"

Dan mopped at his big, work-thinned face. He rubbed his

gaunt and weathered cheek. He sat down on his muddy boot heels and spread the objects before him.

For a long time he gaped at the compact. Finally he opened it and saw powder and rouge. He snapped it shut and turned it over.

"Ghost of Stanley!" whispered Dan. "Shades of Robinson Crusoe. Banquo stalks the sudd. See there! Look, Petey, it's got a big *B* on it. And look there, Petey, those handkerchiefs have *B* on them."

Uneasily his memory stirred within him and he thought dimly about Nairobi without clearly remembering anything definite.

The other packs were put down and Dan saw that they contained clothing and medicine. He found cartridges in the pocket of the shooting jacket and he took them out.

They were for a Mauser Sporting Rifle, 10.75 x 68 mm. A heavy weapon. Hard-nose bullets for elephant.

A phrase hit him, ". . . shells for my ten-seventy-five by sixty-eight . . . Think we'll meet any elephants on Mount Alak?" And then, "Perhaps you'd suggest an air rifle for elephants. I don't believe I've had the pleasure, sir."

The picture of a face, a shoved-back helmet, damp blond curls . . . Such a little kid.

"God," said Dan. "It's . . . it's that girl I saw in Nairobi. Petey! Petey! Throw out the trackers! Pick up that trail. Follow it up. Lippy! Where's my Mauser? Damn you, I'll carry it this time. Sugo! Look after this transit."

"*Bwana,*" said Petey. "Bad luck to follow. She dead by now.

Trail three days old. Porters dump baggage, desert. What about survey?"

"Survey?" said Dan, groggily staring at the compact. "Sure. The survey." Then, with sudden decision, "It can wait for a day or two. Damn it, Petey, she was the most beautiful woman I ever saw and now maybe . . . Let's get going."

Petey now began to repent his haste in bringing his find to his *bwana*. He could just as easily have rubbed out the footprint and thrown these packages into the brush and the work would have gone on as before. Not that Petey had any reason to want the work finished, but it looked safer than chasing off into the marshes where Dinkas and elephants lurked. True to the philosophy which all Africa has in common, Petey was more interested in his own neck than that of a white woman—indeed, he cared very little what happened to any white, save, of course, Dan Courtney, from whom Petey derived his importance.

Petey said, "But, *bwana,* it would be bad to let our men stay idle. They might desert and I do not like to see idle men paid."

Dan, very harassed and tired and irritable, knowing that he did wrong in leaving, whirled on Sugo, the half-caste Arab-Nilote. "Take half the *askaris* and the rod and chainmen and keep heading north on that last reading. I'll pick you up by your stations."

"North?" gaped Sugo, his dark tan face getting gray. "No, no, *bwana*. Not north with *half* the *askaris*. We approach Dinka country. Even now a scout might be watching!"

Dan exploded violently but presently he calmed enough to

say, "All right, damn it, take *all* the *askaris*. I only need Petey and two trackers. And if I find one man missing when I get back, I'll stripe you like a zebra!"

The *askaris* themselves looked rather relieved. They were a sort of police, mercenary soldiers, who wore caps, rifles and cartridge belts but not much else. They were Bagandas, numbering thirty, the safari's men of leisure, who had made up a vanguard ahead with the porters until now.

Petey now saw himself without any company but a pair of trackers and his *bwana* in hostile territory. But he had to bow to his fate, knowing better than to try to start another argument with the engineer.

Dan strode north, snapping at the trackers to hurry and find the place where the loads had been.

# Chapter Three

O N the off chance that he might see something worthwhile with his field glasses, Dan delayed beside the track long enough to scale an anthill. The thing was of the hardness of concrete and was as high as a house, having been painstakingly constructed by a few billion ants who had used their saliva for the glue.

Standing on the crest he focused his glasses to the west, toward the White Nile, which was not far away. At long intervals riverboats might be seen on the stream but there were none now. The White Nile, which was, at this point, some eighteen hundred miles south of Alexandria, offered the only means of travel through the steaming, marshy region. And it was a poor excuse for a thoroughfare. Grass, *um suf,* known as "mother of wool," rose fifteen to twenty feet above the surface of the stream, making long lines of hedgelike obstructions.

Patches of sudd, enormous islands of floating vegetation, which sometimes choked the stream until the riverbed could not be found, could be seen for miles up and down the river.

The only patch of color near at hand was a great bed of waterlilies, red and blue and white, and the only life visible—except for the black flights of mosquitoes and swamp flies—was a whale-headed stork.

Dan mopped his brow, brushing wearily at the insects, and then turned his glasses east. Far away, barely visible through the steamy air, was the telegraph line.

Odd to think that boats on the river passed through this desolate, lonely region. Odder to know that this line of copper wire was carrying news, perhaps this very moment, between Khartoum and Mombasa. Strung on poles more than sixteen feet high (so that the giraffes would not hang themselves and interrupt communication), the wire stretched to infinity, north and south.

But steamers and telegraph line to the contrary, this region was deadly and vicious. The signs of civilization were signs only and somewhere ahead were the Dinka villages, ready to contest the railroad to the last warrior.

Something moved in the reeds. Dan focused his glasses again and sought it out. Finally he glimpsed a naked, tall native, carrying an iron spear, darting from cover to cover along Dan's line of march.

Dan sighed. The Dinkas had picked him up, had they? Damn the Dinkas, the flies, the river, the white rhinos, the steam, the heat. . . .

He slid down the anthill. Ahead of him the trackers were waiting, pointing like a couple of setters at the tracks they had found.

In Bantu, Dan said, "Follow them up! *Run,* don't walk!"

Petey said, "By this time, *bwana,* a buffalo or lioness has probably eaten her. There is no use—"

"Shut up and track," ordered Dan.

At a trot the two trackers followed the trail. It was plain

to see that the girl had been running, as only the toes of her boots had made a mark in most places, very seldom the heel.

The trackers, after they had gone a mile or more, stopped and pointed again.

Dan came up to the spot. The trail widened here and the girl had turned and stood motionless for some time.

"Waiting for something," decided Dan. "All alone. Not even a gun boy. . . ."

Petey reached into the mud and picked up a shell. It was empty, of the caliber 10.75 x 68 mm. Judging by the position of the footprints and the shell, the girl had fired down the trail. The trackers were not able to find blood along the range of vision from the spot.

"Keep going," said Dan.

The trackers trotted off, running their practiced eyes along the trail.

"She must have been half crazy," muttered Dan. "There wasn't anything behind her to shoot at."

"Porters all desert back there," said Petey. "Plenty to shoot at if a porter runs off without his load. Maybe evil spirits trail her."

"She wouldn't run from a spirit," said Dan. "She'd make a stand and slap its face for it."

The trackers were waiting again. They had found a second trail, and by tracing it back a few yards, they discovered that it had been running parallel for some time. They were very ashamed of this oversight and expected instant abuse, but Dan was too worried to give it out.

"Short man," said Petey. "Very thick through. Did not

break many high reeds but break them wide. Deep print. Trail made few minutes after girl pass."

Dan took off his helmet and wiped out the band. Then he swung his Mauser around in front of him and looked into the chamber, making sure it was loaded.

"How old?"

Petey asked the trackers and then said, "Still three days, *bwana*."

"Keep going."

They waded through the reeds and steam and mosquitoes for another hour. And then it became apparent that the girl was tiring. Her steps were unsteady. She would run a few feet and then slow down, staggering.

"Three days ago," whispered Dan to himself.

The trackers were again stopped, this time in the shadow of an anthill. Here the tracks were less distinct, but another empty shell was there, glittering where it had fallen.

The trackers whipped back, ran in circles which grew wider and wider and finally found the marks for which they looked. A spatter of blood, long since blackened, was beside the print of a wide boot.

A heavy man had fallen here, had lain still for some time. The patch deeper in the reeds was wider.

"Good," said Dan. "She nailed the —— in the shoulder. With a three-hundred-and-forty-seven grain slug, she must have torn his goddarned arm off. Good going."

"No, *bwana*," said Petey, who found the remark too hopeful. "Nick in shoulder only. Not enough blood."

28

"Mosquitoes licked it up," said Dan.

"No, *bwana*. Mosquitoes do not eat dead blood, *bwana*. Tracker say man play dead, girl would not come close but go on. Man stop to bind up shoulder, start off east. . . ."

A tracker who had gone on further came back and rattled off a sentence.

"Man still following, *bwana*. Pass night just ahead. Ashes still there." Petey pointed south. "Girl dead by this time, *bwana*. Maybe we better go back."

"Keep going," said Dan. "Find out where the girl went!"

It was growing late in the day and the group had been traveling so fast that they were almost exhausted. All but Dan. No matter how much strength had been drained from him he always seemed to have inexhaustible reserves on which he could call at will. When the trackers hung back he hurled them forward, alternatingly pleading with them and swearing at them.

Dusk was beginning to fall when they found something more alive than footprints.

The trackers had turned a bend in the game trail and were, for an instant, out of sight. Dan swung into the new direction and saw the trackers standing petrified, backs stiff with alarm.

About to swing up his heavy Mauser, Dan heard, "Drop that gun, big guy."

He could see nothing in the reeds. He did not take time. He dived for cover.

A rifle roared. The trackers shrieked and vanished in the

reeds. Petey began to moan hopelessly around the bend, thinking Dan was dead.

"I've got a slug for you any time you want it," said Dan to the invisible bushwhacker.

The rifle roared again, cutting reeds like a scythe over Dan's head.

"Missed me," jeered Dan. "Stand up and try it! Go on, stand up!"

"Wise guy, huh?" said the bodiless voice.

Reeds moved. Dan fired under them.

"You ain't no better, brother. You better stick to your transit!"

"You better stick to bushwhacking," called Dan. "Your name's Bart and your days as a terror to the weaker sex are numbered to about ten minutes. Where's your pal Gotch-ear?"

"Want to know all about it, do you? Keep your nose out of this or I'll feed you some slugs that was built for rhinos."

"Come on over and start feeding any time. What did you do with that girl?"

Bart laughed jerkily. "What's left of her is dead, and that ain't much. What I start out to get, I get. And I shoot to kill. And I love to feed hyenas. Come on, jackal bait. Do you think I've got all night?"

The light was very dim now. It was barely possible to see the tips of the reeds moving against the dark crimson sky. Dan watched carefully.

Presently he began to inch to the right, describing a slow, cautious semicircle which would eventually put him behind Bart.

The world was still.

The sky darkened to indigo.

Dan crept ahead. He was within two yards of where Bart had been. There was nothing there.

Trying to locate the trail away from the spot, on the watch for a glinting gun barrel, Dan lay still, breathing jerkily, his heart pounding against the ground.

Suddenly he grinned. Bart had also moved to the right in a semicircle and was probably now in Dan's former position, coming around in Dan's trail.

Rolling out of the crushed spot and carefully erecting the reeds which would betray his position, Dan turned his rifle toward the place he had quitted.

It was as dark as the inside of a native hut. A few stars were beginning to show faintly. The mist was thickening as the air cooled slightly.

Something rustled not two feet to Dan's left.

He lay still, holding his breath lest it betray him. Bart had done the unexpected. He had come back to the first place he had been, in the hope of forming a second ambush as Dan advanced.

There was a click as Bart took off his rifle's safety. The man, whose breathing could be distinctly heard, expected Dan to crawl into sight in the crushed place.

For several minutes Dan did not move. He could not breathe because Bart would hear that instantly. Dan's lungs were bursting, even though he eased them silently from time to time.

Bart grew impatient. He moved sideways. His foot struck Dan's belt.

With a roar of mingled fear and astonishment, Bart leaped back, trying to bring his heavy rifle to bear.

The barrel swept down and struck Dan's shoulder. Dan shoved under it. The bullet and scorching powder tore at the air over Dan's head and back.

Bart was trying to work his bolt.

Dan snatched the muzzle, jerked it toward him, felt the stock come loose and threw it far to the right.

The movement had taken less than two seconds. Bart had evidently been perfectly willing for the rifle to depart. Steel rasped on leather. Bart had unholstered his automatic.

The pistol stabbed flame through the blackness and whipped down for a second shot.

Dan's Mauser leaped backward as it recoiled. The acrid fumes of smokeless powder boiled upward with the mist.

Bart was slumped on his face, the back blown out of his head.

Stiffly and shakily, Dan got up.

"Petey! Where the hell are you, you coward?"

Petey came, groveling in shame for his ignominious part in the action. Presently the trackers hitched themselves into sight.

With less to be ashamed of, having been almost killed before Dan's arrival, the trackers hastily wrapped up reeds and made torches.

By their light, Dan inspected what was left of the man known as Bart. Dan, while no harder of heart than any other African-schooled engineer, was nevertheless too worked up by the dead man's past pursuit of the girl to spare much regret over his demise.

He rifled the fellow's pockets, since the contents could not be read by hyenas anyway. He did not find very much to identify the man until he opened a small pocketbook.

There, by the smoky light of the torches, he saw a badge pinned on the flap. Under it was a card which was stamped with the name "B. N. Sherman" and signed by Mac-Murray, a man well known in South Africa.

Dan stared for a long time at the badge and then passed a trembling hand over his wet forehead.

"Jesus," said Dan, faintly, "I've killed an IDB cop!"

# Chapter Four

B ECAUSE of the badge, they buried the man known as Bart. It was not a difficult task as the marsh made easy digging. But water kept filling the hole and that delayed them.

When they had finished and had marked the spot with a cross-lashed monument of thorn limbs, Dan Courtney sat on his heels and broke out his pipe.

He smoked a particularly vile brand of Algerian tobacco which was, at best, but partly cured. But if he did not like it, then neither did the mosquitoes and he puffed noisily and industriously and, for a moment, was rid of the squadrons of pests which had been attacking in pursuit formation, doing crash dives.

The trackers, inured to stings and bites, gnawed on some chunks of moldy meat and waited for orders.

"An IDB," muttered Dan. "But why in the hell didn't he sing it out?"

Petey had no answer for this. His round black and white eyes were stabbing the dark reeds beyond the circle of the smoking torches, expecting momentarily a call from roving Dinkas, leopards or lions.

Dan felt very downcast, disillusioned. The canvas was very plain to him now. Gotch-ear, who would sell his grandmother's life for a swig of whiskey, had somehow gotten wind of the girl's and her father's intentions. He had tipped off the IDB and had, undoubtedly for pay, accompanied this fellow Bart on a long trek across the heights of Uganda and into the Sudan sudd.

The identity of the girl and her father had been, until now, very nebulous to Dan. He had supposed that they were just another pair seeking the adventure and thrill of shooting big game. Thanks to the IDB badge, Dan knew that this had merely been a cover for a more profitable, if illegal, scheme.

Kimberley, far to the south, controlled the world's diamond price. That price must be kept up at all costs. But workers, in spite of X-rays, shifted clothing, wire fences and many other devices, sometimes looted rough gems.

The IDB was a special police force which took in hand all crimes involving diamonds.

Perhaps some criminal had stolen a large number of stones at Kimberley or in the Congo and, knowing that escape via the coast was impossible, had headed north the length of the African continent, using the South African railway, the steamers on Lake Tanganyika and Kivu and finally those on the White Nile. It was a natural highway.

This girl's father had come into this region to intercept those stones and take them out under the cover of big game trophies. But Gotch-ear and the IDB . . .

Yes, it was all very plain and Dan regretted exceedingly the gallantry which had led him into the crime of shooting an agent of the IDB. The land here might be without law as to ordinary people, but the killing of the agent would mean jail and a noose in any language.

"I ought to stick to railroads," muttered Dan, disgustedly. "But who the hell would think that such a pretty face could . . ."

He stood up. "On your feet, Petey. Tell the trackers to make another bundle of torches."

Petey bent a little in his dignity, so great was his joy at returning to camp. "Yes, *bwana*. Immediately, *bwana*. It will not be far back to camp. Sugo should have moved directly to the east of us."

"We're not going back to camp."

"*Bwana!*"

"We started in to see what happened to this girl and we'll find out before we sleep again."

"But the dead man said she was also dead, *bwana*."

"There'll be a dead *headman* if you don't snap into it."

"Yes, *bwana*. Immediately, *bwana*."

The trackers hoisted up their *dhotīs*, stuffed the rest of the meat into their mouths and made the torches. They grumbled a little about it until Dan sarcastically remarked that of course only good trackers could work at night and he should have brought better ones.

This acted as a spur to the professional pride of the two natives and they went off at a trot, torches held high and scattering sparks into their wool.

"We'll find out in a minute what turned the IDB around," said Dan. "Tracks any fresher?"

"White man tracks made three hours. Girl tracks maybe two days, maybe more," replied one tracker. "*Kwenda!*"

37

Through the thick, sweaty blackness they proceeded for more than an hour and then the trackers came upon a matter of great interest.

Excitedly they got down on their hands and knees, sniffing and turning and jabbering and arguing and pointing this way and that.

Dan came up. "What is it now?"

"Dinka! Dinka! Dinka!" said one tracker.

"How many?"

"Twice two hands!"

Petey was staring and gulping at a white object in the reeds. Dan rolled it out with his foot.

"Plenty fight," said Petey. "Maybe we better go back to see if Sugo . . ."

Dan examined the human trophy with interest. A big Mauser slug had passed through the lower part of the jaw, leaving very little of the parietal. Although the ants had done a good job of polishing, the bone structure was plain enough to spell Dinka.

The trackers were threshing through the reeds and presently they came in with a battered khaki hat which had a very broad brim and a silk band. Although it was unmarked, the size, twenty-two, clearly indicated that its late owner had been a woman.

One of the scouts now produced a 9 mm Webley automatic pistol of the type issued by the South African Mounted Police. It was already crusted by the damp of the marshes so that it was hard to pull the slide. Dan saw that it had not been fired, which meant that Dinkas had jumped the girl from ambush so quickly that she had only had time to fire one shot from her Mauser rifle before she was overpowered. The pistol, unnoticed, had slipped from its holster as she was being led away.

Dan handed the two items to Petey and then pointed north. "Pick up the Dinka trail."

"*Bwana,*" groaned Petey. "Twice two hands of Dinkas too many. Maybe we better go find Sugo and the *askaris.* She dead by now, *bwana.* Very late. Hard to see tracks. You will lose plenty time on the survey. That Sugo fellow no good, *bwana.*"

"Pick up the tracks," ordered Dan.

The trail was as plain as a riverbed now. Reeds were broken down and crushed flat. Eyes on the ground, the trackers ran swiftly with Dan hard on their heels and Petey jogging in the rear.

About two miles from the Dinka ambush, the trackers found where the IDB man had left the trail to scout ahead. As he had done this, evidently in daylight, with some definite object in view, Dan made the boys swing into the dead man's tracks.

They found a place where the man known as Bart had spent a night. Because the bed was well hidden, Dan knew that he must be within sight of the Dinka village.

He ordered the torches put out and then stood for a long time, listening.

As his eyes grew accustomed to the blackness he began to see the fireflies which swarmed by the millions above the swamp. Their darting, blinking tails shed a greenish glow on the reeds beneath and about them, offering a faint visibility over the soggy terrain.

The trackers did not scout so far ahead now. They were back beside Dan, stepping occasionally to the right and left to turn their flat noses upward and sniff, for all the world like beagle hounds.

Suddenly one of them seized Dan's sleeve and held back, motioning for silence and then pointing straight ahead.

They were under the very walls of a village.

Dan drew back a little, while one tracker located the rickety gate. That done, Dan handed over Bart's cartridges to the trackers and showed them how to load the automatic and the rifle. To Petey he gave the Webley clip.

"When I bust through the gate," whispered Dan, "shoot into the air as fast as you can and yowl like fifty leopards. I want noise. A whole lot of noise."

"Yes . . . b-b-b-bwana," said Petey.

"Ndiyo, bwana, certainly," said the trackers.

Dan slid off the safety of his Mauser and unbuckled the flap of his automatic holster.

He drew back, leaned over and then charged the gate.

The woven fiber sagged and ripped and then collapsed. Dan kicked out of it with his boots.

He shot his rifle skyward and uttered a terrible yell.

Behind him thundered an uproarious volley. The stockade and the grass houses were lit up fitfully by the glare of exploding powder.

With a scream of terror the lately sleeping Dinkas leaped

chattering from their beds. They snatched up spears, thought better of it, piled out of their huts leaving women and children to their fate, and loped in the opposite direction.

Only a handful of the braver warriors jumped down to offer fight. They stood with wide eyes and tensely held spears, halfway between bolting and stabbing.

Dan jerked out his automatic and fired as he ran at them. He saw one go down, then another. He ducked under a spear and slammed a slug into hard flesh.

The warriors fled to a man.

Dan spotted the remains of a fire and snatched a stick out of it, whirling the wood into yellow light.

The firing at the gate stopped as the natives ran out of ready-loaded bullets.

In an instant the whole village would pour back and discover the actual, pitiful number of the attackers.

Dan yelled, "Hello! Hello! Where are you?"

Silence, save for a crying baby, settled down.

"Where are you?" roared Dan, staring round him at the appalling number of mud and grass huts.

Silence again. Not even an echo to his voice. Evidently the task of reloading was proving too complicated for the natives outside.

Dan changed the clip in his pistol, whirled the spark-scattering stick and bore down upon the nearest hut.

He thrust the torch inside. A native woman, teeth chattering in terror, scrambled back away from him to the far side.

Dan tried the next and then the next. A dog with upraised hair set his teeth and snarled.

Another hut and another. A potbellied child looked out of a reed bed, shaking with terror but filled with curiosity.

A tenth and eleventh hut.

A spear zipped out of the night and grazed Dan's hat. He stabbed a shot toward the source and retrieved his headgear.

A fifteenth and sixteenth hut.

Muttering came from the far side of the stockade. The warriors, gathering courage in numbers, were creeping back to investigate and attack.

"Hello!" yelled Dan the hundredth time. "Where are you?"

The twentieth and twenty-first hut gave him no answer.

Three spears sailed across the clearing and pierced the mud and grass hut to Dan's right. He knew the danger of holding that torch any longer but, in his search, he had to have it.

A small, mean dwelling was before him. It would have to be the last before he cut and ran for it. The Dinkas, anxious to retrieve their blighted reputation for courage and fighting ability, now thoroughly awake, would presently circle to cut off the party at the gate.

He ducked through the entrance, thrusting the torch ahead and up. Hastily he scanned the dim interior which was lit but poorly by the smoking flame.

A native woman screamed and pressed back against the far wall. Her lower teeth were missing and she was naked except for a leather apron which shook as she shivered.

Dan backed halfway out the door again. A motion of reeds caught his eye beside the doorway. He glanced that way again. It was nothing but a crudely piled-up bed.

He looked again at the woman. Then he realized that she

was not looking at him but at the reeds, and when Dan turned his own eyes in that direction, he saw that the movement was unmistakable.

A yowl came from the stockade where the warriors, meeting no resistance, were forming a skirmish line to sweep up the invaders. It was high time to be going. Dan backed another step, juggling the automatic in his sweaty palm.

A third time the reeds moved.

With a quick thrust of his boot he scattered the dried grasses.

A white shoulder came to light.

Dan, no longer able to run the risk of the torch, threw it out the door and into the thatch of a hut across the way.

He bent quickly and parted the grass, his hand meeting the laces of a boot and then, shifting quickly, a gag over the face.

With a sudden motion he scooped the girl into his arms. Although she was bound hand and foot he could sense that she was alive. With a feeling of relief he had neither time nor power to analyze, he hugged the girl to his chest.

A spear clanged through the doorway. Dan shifted his burden to his left arm and raised the pistol. He fired twice and then, as the natives drew away, charged out into the stockade, now lighted by the blazing house.

For an instant he was without a sense of direction and then a rifle banged beside the gate. The trackers had finally reloaded.

Running and stopping to fire behind him, Dan made the wrecked entrance and dashed through. The trackers had withdrawn to some distance. A pair of Dinkas swept around the far side of the wall, weapons aloft.

Dan turned and deliberately planted his last two shots.

*Dan shifted his burden to his left arm and raised the pistol.*

The natives fell. An ivory armlet rolled into the light of the blazing hut and gyrated to a stop.

With a yell for Petey, Dan raced out into the reeds.

When they were a few hundred yards away, Dan stopped long enough to put another clip into his automatic and then empty it at the glowing sky behind him.

Then, with pursuit discouraged, they headed southeast toward the place where Sugo and the *askaris* should be.

As they went, Dan unlashed the girl's bonds and gag, but her head hung limply back and the one arm which was free swung from side to side each time Dan took a step.

He wondered why the slackly swinging hand made him feel so afraid; why, now that the danger was over, he should be so afraid and worried.

Gently carrying her as though she was a china doll which the slightest jar would break, Dan walked through the black and steaming night, upset and content all at one and the same time.

# Chapter Five

THE west paled into dawn before Dan crossed the line where the stakes and stations should have been. But they were not there.

He was not immediately apprehensive. It was possible that Sugo had been unable to run out a five-mile line in what had remained of yesterday.

On compass, then, with Petey mumbling all manner of ghastly prophecies as to the fate of the camp, they backtracked the line.

One mile, two miles, three miles, and still no Sugo. Dan was beginning to stagger from hunger, thirst and weariness. The trackers began to exchange meaning looks and Petey's wail grew more audible.

The girl, who at first had been so light, was now definitely a burden and Petey, seeing that his *bwana*'s strength had already outlasted anything humanly possible to his way of thinking, began to hint that the girl, who was probably dying anyway, had better be left beside the trail.

Dan did not seem to gather the drift of Petey's remarks and Petey, growing bolder and more frightened than ever at the prospect of being left without the protection of a powerful *bwana* in this desolate and hostile waste, finally said, "But she is dead, *bwana*. She must be. See, I touch her half-opened eyes and she does not blink. I—"

Dan, with a well-placed jab of his rifle muzzle, knocked Petey flat on his back in the muck.

Aggrieved by such treatment, the *mnyapara* nursed his woes thereafter in the rear.

The man had unfortunately voiced Dan's worst fears. The girl's face was as white as rice powder and her lips were blue, as though she was very cold. From time to time he anxiously felt of her wrist, but his clumsy, numb fingers could feel no throb of life below the delicate skin.

Three miles, four miles, five miles.

They came upon the tracks which they had found the day before and located the last station which had been made. Dan glared at the inoffensive scrap of paper and snarled a monotonous chain of profanity.

They went down the line of stakes. The camp should have been there, but it was not. The scattered remains of the broken transit lay where the white rhino had tossed them. The packages Petey had found had been ripped apart and the girl's clothing was strewn about in disorder.

Dan made Petey spread out a piece of the canvas and then stake a shade over it. On this rough bed he placed the girl.

After a worried look at her face and a futile effort to chafe some warmth into her hands, he realized he had neither whiskey nor medicine and could do nothing else.

The trackers slumped wearily on their haunches. Petey, with a sigh, stretched out in the mud. Dan looked into his automatic to see if it was loaded and then showed it to Petey.

"Look well," said Dan, "because I am traveling. And if you have moved an inch when I get back, the next time you see this gun it will be letting some of the yellow out of you. Understand?"

"But *bwana* . . ."

"Stay here!"

Dan searched around inside himself and wondered if he had nerve enough to go on now that his energy was spent. He supposed that he had and, with a glare at the three, strode back along the line.

The tracks he found were all fresh. Some of them did not even have water in them, so recently had they been made. By shutting his jaw tight and concentrating hard he kept the solar system of spots, which danced along ahead, from blinding him.

He might have been more cautious if he had stopped and examined the spoor more closely. But it was all he could do to keep in motion and he was afraid to stop, not knowing if he could start again.

The boys were all in line, evidently, moving as fast as porters can be expected to move. It failed to occur to Dan that it would take more than weak-spined Sugo to keep these natives in marching file. Otherwise there would be stragglers, lost loads and the main group would be bunched up.

He followed until the sun was high and scorching, until the steam rose like uncountable ghosts over the flat and dismal landscape.

An anthill had been skirted by the deserting safari. Dan ran solidly into it and stood by, staring at it. Presently he reasoned that it would be best to climb it and, slowly, he hitched himself to the lopsided top.

Less than a thousand yards ahead he saw the sun slide greasily from the backs of porters. If he had not seen it, it is likely that he could not have forced himself forward. He had been constantly on the march for thirty hours and for a good ten hours of that time he had been carrying the girl.

He found another reservoir of energy and realized what it would mean if he were stranded here without food or shelter in the land of the Dinkas. Rage flared up within him.

He slid down off the anthill, threw a big cartridge into his Mauser chamber and set off at a jog trot.

With the sweat streaming from him and his wind like a knife in his throat, Dan caught sight of the last man in line. The fellow was an *askari,* marching in good order to pick up stragglers.

Dan overtook him. The *askari* whirled in alarm at the sound of steps behind and when he saw what he supposed to be a departed spirit, he screamed loud and long.

Loads avalanched to the ground. Porters dived hastily into the reeds. *Askaris* nervously wondered whether to stand and die or run and live.

Sugo, somewhere near the center of the column, glanced back in midair and recognized Dan. He was educated enough to know he couldn't see a ghost that plain and he instantly popped back into view with a glad shout.

*"Bwana!"*

Heads jumped up like a hundred native Punches. Eyes rolled white. Ashamed, now that Sugo assured them, the porters came into sight and sheepishly fumbled about for their loads.

Part of the column was around a turn in the reeds and now these came back to look and see for themselves.

Swearing in English, Swahili, Bantu and Dutch, Dan waded through them, knocking them to the right and left, bawling at them to turn around and get in line.

His tirade was split apart by the roar of a .300 Scott rifle.

A porter on Dan's right was whirled twice about before he was slammed to earth with a bullet through his heart.

Dan dropped hastily down on one knee and swung his sights toward the sound. He could see reeds waving and he took a chance shot high into them.

The sound of a man floundering through the marsh was heard and Dan stood up to follow.

Two hundred yards away something moved beside an anthill and Dan sent dust geysering away from the towering mound. An instant later he saw a big-shouldered, round-headed man dive from behind it and into the reeds again.

Dan placed a third shot for luck. He was too tired to follow into a possible trap. He had to think of other matters. That one glimpse had told him that the man was Gotch-ear!

With the help of Sugo, Dan hauled the porters into view again. They buried the dead native—with very little emotion on the part of his late fellows—and then formed in line.

Refreshed by a drink of boiled water into which he had poured a stiff jolt of whiskey and quinine, Dan started them north.

"Soooo sorreee!" apologized Sugo, helping Dan along.

"*Askari* follow you up, pretty soon hears shots, come back quick. Before dawn big white *sahib* walk in on us and say you plenty dead. He say he's good friend *Bwana* Courtney, come to take us back to Soroti so we not get killed by Dinkas. And he say if we not go, he plenty use pistol on us. So, what can we do? *Askari* and white both say *bwana* dead."

"Don't let it happen again," growled Dan. "Whether I'm dead or alive, you follow orders. That fellow had part of his ear gone, didn't he?"

"You see him far off and notice—? Good eyes, *bwana*. Yes, part of his ear chewed off."

"Was he carrying anything? A package of some sort?"

"No, *bwana*. While he eat breakfast I look very close. Nothing on him but rifle and pistol, *bwana*. We go ahead with line?"

"Yes. You're damned right we go ahead."

"Dinka country and all?"

"Dinka country, high water, blizzards and devils, the survey goes through. Now shut up."

"Yes, *bwana*."

# Chapter Six

THE new, additional responsibility of the girl's well-being played havoc with big Dan Courtney's reason. He was caught between two accusing fingers—he must make the girl pull through and he knew that he was willingly harboring a criminal. These two made a neat balance, but to them was added a force so mysterious that Dan could not bring it into the glare of light. Faced for the first time was a certain feeling of awe and reverence for her, the crying need to protect her and make her well again.

A quest of the back trail proved that the remainder of her safari had vanished as though swallowed by the White Nile. Only a handful of her porters had been pried out of foxholes by Dan's *askaris* and these were too stunned and starved to be of help in locating the rest. The necessity to push on and the constant danger of massed attack from the Dinkas forbade a more thorough search.

Out of a safari which had numbered more than a hundred Bantu and two whites, only eight natives and the girl, Barbara, seemed to be alive. But even such wholesale disaster did not much affect the emotions of the men—who were principally concerned with getting through the dangerous region and getting back home again—alive.

The matter would, of course, be reported to the District

Commissioner—some weeks' travel from there—and a report would be entered in the files. That was all. Regrettable, of course. But as it would take a British Army Corps to thoroughly subdue the Dinkas, nothing could be done.

The matter of the dead IDB man, thought Dan, would be somewhat more trying. This fellow Gotch-ear might get out of the country alive and he might know what had happened to the fellow known as Bart. The District Commissioner would not be at all concerned, but the IDB, reaching around the world and back again, with the fate of the world's diamonds in their hands, would probably ferret out the answer.

And that, for Dan, would be very fatal.

Assured that the girl would live and fully recover and that blackwater fever played no part in her illness, Dan kept his line going at full speed.

It was necessary to move camp each and every day. They had taken their last curve until they came close to the Bahr el Azraq—the Blue Nile—when they would swerve to tie in with the Anglo-Egyptian railhead at Sennar.

Dan checked the line a mile at a sight. Someday, when trains came flashing through from Mombasa to Khartoum, they would be able to open the throttle and hold it open for fifty miles at a stretch.

It was not harmful to the girl to be carried in a gently borne hammock slung from a long pole and though Dan would hover around the netting of her bed, anxiously wondering if he couldn't do something for her ten times a day, he had already done his bit.

After a week of this, during which time they had rolled

up fifty-three miles of stakes across the marshy flats, the shock-produced coma had begun to wear away. And then, one dawn while Dan sat wearily and sleepily over his coffee, Petey came to his tent.

"She talk," said Petey.

Dan was instantly alive. He went quickly to her shelter, zipped up the talon-clasped net and went in.

The girl was propped up a little by a blanket, and though her face was thin and her lack of strength apparent, she had smoothed back the blond curls in an effort to look better.

She stared curiously at Dan, trying to remember where she had seen him. Then, smiling, she whispered, "Air rifles . . . on elephants."

Dan sat down beside her. "No talking now. You pulled through but you didn't have much room to spare. You're in good hands, though there isn't another white woman within two hundred miles. Is there anything I can do for you?"

She moved her head a little and then whispered, growing tense, "Where's Dad?"

Dan stared studiously at a fly which was walking up the netting outside.

"He's . . . ?"

Dan looked back to her. "He probably trekked back to Soroti. Only eight of your natives were around when we picked you up. Yes, that's it. He's on his way back."

"He wouldn't leave me. He's dead!"

"Please," begged Dan. "Don't get excited. You need your strength. Ahead there's probably a village and if he didn't trek back he went north. Wherever he is, we'll know about

55

it pretty soon. We searched hard for your baggage and men and we didn't find any . . . well, any dead."

"Then the Dinkas have got him, the way . . ."

"We'll know about it pretty soon. You better go back to sleep."

"Are we close to where . . . ?"

"To be exact, we're fifty-three miles two thousand and twenty feet from the place we picked you up. I'm sorry, but I'm surveying a railroad and I'm pushed for time. You've been carried from camp to camp and you'll be moved again today."

"Yes, . . . Yes, of course."

The talk had taxed her greatly and she was asleep a moment later. A frown had wearily crept around her tired eyes.

Much as he might have wanted to linger there until she was strong enough to be up and about, Dan was forced to pick up and thrust forward another eight miles that day.

The girl knew nothing at all about it, as Dan had promised to reward her hammock bearers with a stripe for every jolt and the country along the White Nile basin changed but little, so that when she sat up again that evening, it appeared to her that she had not moved a yard.

That day was a trying one. Dan ran into difficulties when he wanted them the least. A noon sight with his transit told him that they had arrived at 11°39'15" north latitude, 33°30'12" east longitude. A short distance to the north he knew he would find the village where Stephans had been killed while engaged on this same mission.

From the account of an escaped *askari*, Stephans had tried to see the *Bain* of Kurfung, the most powerful, at present, of the Dinka strongholds. He had been granted an audience but had been ambushed and speared with most of his men on his way to keep the appointment.

Dan now understood why that interview had been necessary. At this point he found a morass stretching for miles to the east and west and long hours spent in sounding the slime revealed that it seemed to have no solid bottom.

Except in one place, only the amphibious crocs could navigate this sea of muck. Dan found that place, a sort of ridge of solid ground running north and south, heading directly toward Kurfung and touching solid ground at the very stockade gates of the Dinka capital.

He knew this from the strike, although the Dinka town was more than twelve miles away and out of sight in the steamy air.

Much troubled, he caused camp to be pitched on the edge of the soggy ground near the ridge he hoped to use. He had slaved in the mud and fought the insects which rose out of the rotting reeds like thunderheads until his nerves were on the razor edge, and that night he sat gloomily in his tent and hopelessly surveyed the situation.

He had come so far and through so much that to be balked now would be a bitter dose to take. He had too few *askaris* to attempt an attack upon the place. Unlike the village where he had found the girl, Kurfung was surrounded by a mud wall as hard as concrete, impossible to climb. At least a thousand warriors were in the place.

His one consolation was the fact that the camp could not be jumped as long as he held the narrow span of the ridge.

Only a few Dinkas could come over that at a time and a few well-placed shots could drive them back.

His gloom deepened, the more he thought about it. Some engineer! he told himself sarcastically. Scant regard he'd had for his job this trip.

He'd killed an IDB for which he would eventually have to answer. He had attacked a Dinka town and killed several warriors. He had almost lost his safari to a man. He was, no matter his own feelings, harboring a person who must be very much wanted by the IDB. And when he piled all these ugly matters up on the table before him and stared moodily at them, he read failure, possible death, at best, a long delay.

But the next day he tried to find another ridge with renewed determination, not moving his camp. And for the following eight days he continued his useless search, growing more weary and irritable than ever. A touch of malaria was not helping any and he would stand in the searing sunlight and alternately freeze and bake.

Finally he was convinced he could do nothing but cross the ridge, straight toward Kurfung, and battle it out with the men who had killed Stephans and wiped out the Lawry party. He returned to camp with that decision gnawing at him.

When he had changed his soggy clothing for clean khaki, he ordered up a slug of quinine and whiskey and sprawled, exhausted, in his hammock.

A shout which pierced the dusk an instant later brought him scrambling to his feet and snatching up his battery, but evidently the *askaris* had the matter in hand as soon as it had happened.

Two very important natives, with rifles ready, were prodding a Dinka down the line of tents toward Dan's. The whole camp joined in the procession and everybody talked at the same time.

The *askaris* made the captive halt outside Dan's netting.

The Dinka looked very haughty. He was almost six feet tall and well built. He had a thin, cruel mouth and a sharp nose which contrasted strangely with the blackness of his face. He was dressed in three ivory armlets and a loincloth. He glared as he awaited his doom.

As Dan could not speak the Sudanic tongue, he had to talk through the all-knowing Petey.

"Ask him what he's doing here."

Petey got the answer and said, "He come to look over how many we are. The *askaris* find him coming out of the swamp."

"Ask him who his chief is."

Petey garnered, "Chief very big man. Plenty warriors. Biggest *Bain* in Dinka country. He say chief gobble up white man in one bite. Plenty powerful, plenty strong."

Dan had no reason to doubt this. He knew that a Dinka chief holds office only as long as he is in perfect health and great strength. When either fails, it is up to the tribe to kill their *Bain*.

"Tell him we are going to go through the country and that we'll kill anyone who tries to stop us."

Petey relayed this but only a straighter spine showed that the Dinka had heard. Presently Petey had an answer.

"He say he know. He say *Bain* not want steel trail through his land. He say *Bain* already kill two other whites and can kill a hundred more if necessary."

"What's the name of this *Bain*?"

Petey presently had, "He say Great Devil or something like that. Plenty powerful Dinka, he say."

"Ask him why this Great Devil does not want the railroad to go through here," said Dan.

"He say," Petey found out, "that *Bain* say railroad very bad for Dinka. Bring bad crops and sick people. And he say you already kill a lot of Dinkas south of here and he plenty mad about that. He say you come closer to Kurfung and *Bain* kill everybody. Maybe I think we better—"

"I don't give a damn what you think. Tell this fellow to go back and tell his rainmaker that I am going to go through past Kurfung. Tell him I have thirty rifles and if he stops me there'll be a lot more dead Dinkas. Tell him I don't give a tinker's damn for all the Dinkas above the equator. Tell him I eat a Dinka every morning before breakfast."

When this was told to the native, he looked very disdainfully up and down Dan's tall height and then, with great contempt, spat as close to the boots as he dared.

Dan kept his temper. "Kick him out of camp."

When the Dinka had been dragged away, Petey whined, "He mean that, *bwana*. You get killed sure if we go another step. Don't—"

"When I want your advice, you'll know about it," snapped Dan. "Double the guard all around and keep a fire going all night. Now see that I get something to eat."

# Chapter Seven

HE must have dozed a while before his dinner was ready because when he woke up he thought he was still dreaming.

The girl Barbara was sitting at his table, waiting for him.

Dan came fully awake. He stood up and grasped the back of a canvas chair and looked down at her, across the table.

"You ought to be in bed," said Dan.

"I'm more fit than you are," said the girl. "You look like your own ghost. Sit down and have a slab of this eland steak. It smells wonderful."

"My *mpishi* never had a hand in cooking that," grinned Dan. "It looks edible."

"I assure you, he did."

"And I assure you he didn't. Look here . . . Miss Barbara . . . you've only been in bed ten days. . . ."

"Three weeks," she corrected him.

"Well, have it your way. How do you feel?"

"Swell."

"Why, my God," said Dan, "you're a Yank!"

"No less."

"I ought to say it's a small world or something," said Dan.

"Don't. Sit down before you fall down."

"Aw, I just need a couple hours' sleep, that's all. I been walking around poking sticks in the mud for a week."

"And you found you had to use the ridge toward Kurfung. Your *mnyapara*, Petey, has been telling me about it."

"He runs off at the mouth something fierce," said Dan, cutting the tender meat. "Don't believe anything he tells you."

"Maybe not. Tell me, Mr. Courtney, did you pick any of my battery out of the trail? I had the ten-seventy-five to which you objected and a .300 Scott magazine rifle and a pretty little sixteen-gauge Scott Premier shotgun. The 9 mm Webley automatic pistol—"

"If you want a good battery," said Dan, "I've got a Mauser ten-seventy-five I . . . er . . . picked up. I've got your Webley and I can give you a Remington shotgun. With luck we may find the rest someday. By the way, you've just claimed the former possession of about two thousand bucks' worth of armament. You ought to be more careful of such expensive things. You shouldn't go throwing them away. What's all the interest in your battery?"

"Petey *does*, as you say, run off at the mouth, Mr. Courtney. I may be the partial cause of this coming show with the Dinkas, and I'm no Lady Achilles to sulk in my netting."

He looked at her intently. She was a very unusual person, this Barbara. She had a sweet, boyish little face, a very pert nose, a small but generous mouth and a pair of very frank eyes which were blue or violet or maybe green—he couldn't tell by the lantern light. She didn't come up to his shoulder and yet she was sitting there casually discussing a scrap which would be a very bombastic and dangerous affair.

No, Dan decided, he had never seen anything like her. Most women, when they hunted big game, expected you to hold their rifle while . . . But come to think of it, he had never known many of these great ladies. Now this girl, Barbara . . . With a shock he remembered that an IDB man had been very close on her trail, intent upon her capture. He couldn't believe it, looking at her now.

After a while a servant took away the plates and for a long time the couple sat across the board from each other with little to say. But they discovered there was no reason to say anything and with that came the realization to them both that this was far from a casual meeting, that this was not the last time it would happen.

Finally, saying that he needed rest, she stood up to go. He was instantly on his feet.

"Remember, if there's to be a show . . ." she said.

"You're . . . that's . . . well, it's swell of you," said Dan. "But I don't think we'll have a lot of trouble."

She stepped to the tent and zipped the fastener open and stood for an instant looking out at the billions of fireflies which flashed in the dark. Then she turned her head a little and told him good night and was gone.

Dan sat down on his hammock and grinned without any visible reason. He stretched lazily, and contentedly hummed a bar or two of a half-forgotten song. He started to call for his boy and a nightcap, but he closed his mouth and looked down at his boots.

He sat that way for a long time. Gradually the drone of the camp simmered down to an occasional sleepy grunt.

At last Dan pulled his automatic from its holster and slowly inspected the clip.

"If I could do it . . . It wouldn't be murder. Not after Stephans and Lawry. . . ."

He put the pistol back and looked again at his boots. He knew he could not let Barbara in for a scrap with the Dinkas. He knew he could tarry no longer in this camp. Time was short enough and he had to get the survey through.

He made a movement as though he was flipping a coin and pretended to read its fall. "All or nothing," he said with decision.

He ripped a leaf out of his recording book and scribbled a note upon it. Then he put on his helmet and buckled a cross of cartridge belts over his shoulders. He picked up his Mauser and fed the magazine.

As he reached up to turn out the gasoline lantern he again looked at the note.

> Dear Barbara,
>
> I'm taking a walk tonight. If I am not back here by the time you read this, take command of this safari and head back for Soroti. The boys will be very willing to go. Although it is close to seven hundred miles, you'll find my stakes the whole way and the going is all good. If you want, try to stab east for the coast and get out by Mogadishu in Italian Somaliland. You can avoid the IDB that way. Here's luck. Goodbye.
>
> Dan Courtney

He turned the lantern out.

# Chapter Eight

PETEY was sleeping the sacred sleep of an important headman and his snores were quite as loud as the roars of a lion somewhere in the highlands beyond.

A terrific nightmare entered his woolly head. A rhino charged him with lowered horn. The rhino's head scooped skyward, carrying Petey ferociously through the air.

But just at the instant Petey landed, he sat up yowling and staring about for the rhino and wailing for his *bwana*.

"Shut up, you fool," said Dan. "Get up. You're going on a trip."

Petey saw that it was Dan's boot and not a rhino horn which had gored him and his relief was so great that he was instantly on his feet and ready to leave.

Sugo was snoozing close by and Dan jarred him into wakefulness. "Sit up and listen," ordered Dan.

Rubbing his eyes and muttering sleepily, Sugo collected his far-flung wits and did as he was told.

"I'm taking a walk north," said Dan.

Sugo came to himself wholly and completely and gaped at his *sahib*, wondering if Dan had suddenly gone mad.

"You will remain here," Dan continued. "If I am not back in a reasonable length of time—say tomorrow noon—you will be under the orders of the white *memsahib*. You will move south with adequate precautions against a Dinka ambush and return to Uganda or any place the lady may direct. Colonel Malone will be ready to pay you off on call at Soroti or Nairobi."

Sugo was too stunned to say anything. Convinced that he was still asleep, he blinked and opened and closed his mouth after the fashion of a croc with indigestion.

Petey, meantime, had taken all this in. He said, "We make sure white lady get back, *bwana*."

"You," said Dan, "can speak Sudanic and I need you with me."

"Oooooh, *bwana*, I have wives and many children and am their sole support. Oooooh, *bwana*, I cannot—"

"Take your choice," said Dan. "You get a Dinka spear in your chest or a 9 mm slug in your back. What will it be?"

Petey instantly saw that the spear was less certain than the slug. He had imposed upon Dan with his questionable services long enough to know his *bwana*. When Dan looked like his face was carved out of granite and when he held his left hand in a fist and when his eyes were so narrow that it was impossible to tell whether they were green like a cat's or blue like the sea, Petey did not argue.

Slumped over under his burden of dismal woe, Petey shuffled toward the ridge which led toward Kurfung. Convinced his *bwana* had suddenly gone mad, he promised himself a quick dive into the reeds at the earliest opportunity.

Dan knew that it was useless to explain his motives. The mathematics of his reasoning could be put into a simultaneous equation which involved theory, to say nothing of integral calculus.

He did not need his slipstick to work out the answers. Dan squared plus one Webley times muzzle velocity times a one-hundred-and-ten grain lead and steel slug equaled one Dinka *Bain* disintegrated. And as he walked silently along away from camp and into the north he kept saying to himself,

$$ "D^2 + W \times V \times 110s = \frac{df}{dy} dDB." $$

But as Petey did not happen to be an engineer, he would not have understood.

Dan, pushing through reeds as silently as a big cat, watching and listening for any Dinka scout, also knew the other equation. One Dinka *Bain* plus one thousand warriors squared times one thousand sharp spears plus one mud stockade divided by one Dan might equal one engineer disintegrated.

After traveling more than five miles in two hours, with his face cut by grass and his boots caked with mud, he recalled uncomfortably that one Dinka *Bain* plus one thousand warriors had already reduced Stephans and Lawry to one over infinity, a fraction so small as to be wholly nonexistent.

Petey, all this while watching his chance, was still kept going by Dan's close watch. Petey, having been raised in this land of dark and brooding mystery, had known Dinkas by reputation since his birth. His mother used to frighten him into obedience by telling him that the Dinkas would get him and he began to suspect that his mother had not been far from wrong.

The swamp, aglow with shimmering clouds of fireflies, was weird and depressing. Crocs occasionally bellowed in the direction of the river and once a lion told the shivering world that he had made a kill and was duty-bound to protect it. But as this lion was far away on drier, higher land, Petey need not have let his teeth beat tempo to the hunting song of the brute.

Two more hours, according to the glow of Dan's wristwatch, had passed when they came to the end of the ridge. By calculation the Dinka village was still some distance ahead, but according to mathematics, a guard would be somewhere in the vicinity, ready to give the alarm in case the survey party sought to pass.

Dan shoved Petey into cover in the damp mud and thrust a handkerchief between Petey's teeth to stop their castaneting. And now, where was the Dinka?

Dan crawled ahead for twenty yards, turned to the right as silently as a stalking leopard, turned again and came south, back toward Petey.

Something clinked ahead of him.

Dan stopped on all fours, gripped his automatic by the muzzle, and listened intently.

The clink came again. A dozen air corps of fireflies searchlighted the spot for an instant. Something black and gleaming was seated five feet away.

Now the question was, how to approach soundlessly and deliver the coup before the Dinka could raise the alarm.

Dan moved a few inches and paused again. The blinking bugs showed the gleam a second time. Dan came slowly to his feet.

He leaned forward as though falling, holding the pistol butt aloft.

He caught a gleam of white teeth and eyeballs. The Dinka had sensed his doom. The mouth opened to shout.

The only sound in the steaming night was the thump of steel into matted wool.

Dan laid the Dinka out and found that he still breathed. Making a vine into a rope, Dan tied the fellow's hands behind him and then gagged him with a strip torn from the fellow's loincloth.

Dan slid back to find Petey.

The hole in the mud was there, still warm. So was Dan's handkerchief.

But of Petey there was no sign. By now he was three miles on his way back across the ridge, going so fast that his hard heels floated a whole yard above the ground, splitting the air with a fear-distended nose.

Dan swore silently to himself and then turned back to his captive. The man was still dreaming about buying another dozen wives with a couple dozen cows and again Dan left him, to slide around in the brush in a search for another guard.

About a hundred feet from the spot, he ran into a whole nest of Dinkas. He almost placed his hands on a gently heaving chest.

Crab-fashion he backed up.

The guard there was dozing peacefully, sitting upright, surrounded by two dozen of his fellows.

Dan saw no reason to disturb this lazy scene. The fight would be too noisy. Of course, when these fellows changed the guard on the ridge, they would find their fellow gone.

They would conclude a hungry crocodile had gotten him and then would remember that he had not yelled, and shortly after that the whole outfit would descend upon Kurfung shouting murder, blood and death.

By that time Dan hoped he would have his work done.

He slid back and threw the senseless Dinka scout over his shoulder and, proceeding as softly as a shadow, went forward toward Kurfung.

# Chapter Nine

B Y daylight Kurfung looked like the children of the giants had been playing a careless game of mud pies. At night, with a few smoldering fires still flickering within the wide limits of the ant-concrete wall, the red-daubed domes gave it the appearance of a genie metropolis straight out of the Arabian Nights.

Although almost every other smell was blotted out by the odiferous discord of Dan's burden, Dan could still get a whiff or two which spelled rotting meat and a none-too-complete system of sewage.

Evidently this friendly odor of the town served as smelling salts to the trussed guard. He began to wiggle, and as he weighed close to two hundred pounds, the movement was inconvenient.

Dan dumped the native on the ground and shoved his Webley into a tender section of the fellow's ribs.

Although Dan could speak no Sudanic, Bantu—mixed with Swahili and a little Masai, and flavored with a strong shot of Madi—could be made to serve as a medium of thought exchange. Repeating his order variously, Dan gave the Dinka to understand that the location of the *Bain*'s dwelling place was greatly desired.

The Dinka could not talk through his gag and Dan did

not dare remove it and the only solution lay in letting the Dinka lead the way at a walk.

At first the Dinka padded slyly toward the gate but Dan, as soon as he saw the portals a hundred feet ahead, discouraged the effort, making the man understand that he must find a way over the wall.

The Dinka pretended great ignorance of any such ingress, pointing at the concrete-like mud and shaking his head.

He was getting nowhere with this method and Dan changed his tactics. He had saved a length of vine and with it he carefully lashed the native's ankles together. Then he propped the Dinka up against the flat side, carefully showed him that it was possible to fire straight down with the Webley, and made use of his human steppingstone.

The Dinka knew better than to oppose this effort. Dan stepped on the V formed by the lashed wrists, stepped up on the slippery shoulders and reached skyward for the top of the wall. His fingers closed on a pointed stick set into the structure.

He doubled up his knees and launched himself upward to the crest and steadied himself there. By the same movement the Dinka was thrown flat on his face.

Dan, supposing that the native could not travel far while so securely bound, dropped twelve feet down to the ground inside Kurfung.

There was but small activity in the place. A few fires smoldered. A few Dinkas were gathered around these spots of red here and there, but, on the whole, the dark metropolis slept.

Stepping softly, Dan made his way along the backs of a row of huts, pausing every few feet to look about him.

With a thoroughness which smacked of years spent back of a transit, he surveyed Kurfung, comparing the sizes of the dwellings in an effort to find the most likely throne room of the *Bain*.

A dog caught his scent and charged him, growling.

Dan scooped the animal off the ground and jabbed a wrist down the wet, sticky throat. Considerably startled, the dog tried to claw free but before this could be done, Dan's handkerchief was sacrificed to the cause. The jaw was clamped shut and the bit of cloth was tied around the muzzle.

Unable to do more than whimper about it, the dog was allowed to go away.

The noise of the disturbance had been slight. On the other side of the compound two hounds were evidently at war with each other.

Dan slid onward, grinning slightly, rather pleased with his success so far. A moment later he had spotted a big dwelling which was unmistakably the *Bain*'s.

He went to the side door of his goal and bent over to look in. The interior was dark and odorous and generally repulsive.

Dan stepped inside, feeling before him with his left hand, carrying his Webley in his right.

He contacted the bottom of a reed-covered bed, slid his fingers up the rustling length of it and touched warm flesh.

But he could not be sure that this was the *Bain* himself. It might be a servant or a wife.

73

Dan had to take the chance. The sleeper stirred uneasily. Dan reached into his pocket for a match.

The rest of his plan would soon be complete. While he had no compunctions about blowing out the brains of the man who had murdered Stephans and Lawry, a shot inside Kurfung would seal his own doom.

All he had to do now was knock the *Bain* out, tie him up and pack him out of Kurfung and back to camp where, at leisure, he could hold the ridge against all attack and use the *Bain* as a wedge for peace.

He drew the match case out, unscrewed the cap, selected a wooden stick and pulled it forth.

Dan was about to strike it on the mud floor when all hell broke loose at the gate!

The shouts which soared up and out into the night were echoed along the line. Within a space of ten seconds, Dan believed the whole village was giving tongue.

The Dinka scout, by rolling, had at last reached the main gate and the guards!

The sleeper came awake with a roar which resembled a cornered lion's snarl and leaped up so suddenly that he struck Dan.

On the instant, the *Bain* realized that he did not hold a Dinka. Dinkas did not wear cartridge belts or shirts.

Dan slammed a right into the *Bain*'s chest and sent the fellow reeling. A cudgel swished out of the dark and crashed into Dan's shoulder.

From the *Bain*'s throat there burst a long, imperious yell.

Again Dan connected a fist with a chest. Abruptly he

realized that his Webley was somewhere on the floor. He stepped savagely into the fray and let the *Bain* have a rapid one-two in the face.

Warriors were thundering up to the rescue, crowding into the door, reaching eagerly into the darkness.

Dan fought his way back into a corner. They could tell him from the others by the slightest touch of his clothing.

Before a light could be brought, the black avalanche had Dan down on the mud floor, holding him with sheer weight and manpower. They wrenched away the rifle which was slung over his back. Scrambling fingers found the Webley. Disarmed and subdued, Dan found he could not do more than blink and wonder what would happen next.

A torch flickered smokily through the door. The red haze of light sent the black shadows writhing along the walls.

The *Bain* was not in the crowd. He was seated on a chair which was set on a mud pedestal three feet off the ground. He was swathed in a cloak of lion skins and he wore a grinning devil mask.

Through the ghoulish visage came a clacking rattle of Sudanic. Dan was lifted roughly to his feet and held strenuously.

Hoping the *Bain* knew Madi, Dan said, "I did not know the Dinkas were governed by such a weakling. If your warriors had not come I would have held you powerless with one hand."

At first hearing, his words appeared very foolhardy. If he did not antagonize them he might have a chance. But Dan had an excellent reason for what he said.

"I am disappointed," he yelled in Madi. "I had thought

the Dinkas were great and now I find that their rainmaker is sickly and limp with weakness."

A snarl from the devil mask sought to stem the rush of his words, but Dan, taking no chance on Madi, slammed out the same substance in Bantu, making the words rattle like machine-gun fire.

The *Bain* roared orders at the warriors. The natives set their heels and hands and dragged Dan out the door and into the darkness.

Yowling and prancing about him, jabbing at him with spears, they harried Dan into another hut of mean proportions and catapulted him across the inside to the hard, unyielding wall beyond. He tangled his feet in something soft and when he whirled he saw crossed spears silhouetted against the glow outside.

Posting three warriors of excellent reputation, the Dinkas whirled away to lie about it and their parts in it to the rest of the village.

Dan reached down to see what had tripped him and felt a shoulder clothed in a tattered shirt.

A gentle English voice said, "Who are you?"

# Chapter Ten

A S his eyes grew accustomed to the dim light which came from the leaping rebuilt fires in the compound, Dan recognized the old and seasoned gentleman of Nairobi.

"Your daughter is back with my safari," said Dan. "She's all right and looking well. She can get out of here with my *askaris*."

As no man who has been hardened in the mold of Africa shows much emotion, the old man nodded and said, "Thanks."

"I suppose they brought you and your porters up here to Kurfung after they jumped you," said Dan.

"Yes. You're the surveyor for the railroad, aren't you?"

"I was," said Dan.

"Pretty excited about something, aren't they?"

"Sounds that way," said Dan, stretching out on the dry reeds. "I haven't slept much lately. Do you mind?"

"Not at all. I'll wake you up if anything happens."

Dan, having reached that point of mental and physical exhaustion which makes the body writhe and plead for slumber, and feeling no uncertainty now as to his immediate fate, dozed off.

It was bright daylight and very hot when he woke up. His clothes were sticking to him and his hair was damp against his forehead.

77

He planted his heels apart and rested his elbows on his knees and stared moodily out through the doorway.

"Still pretty excited," said the haggard old man, sitting against the wall.

"Yeah," said Dan, listening to the rumpus. "Wonder what's the delay."

"Takes time to fix up a party, I suppose."

"I suppose so."

Conversation languished for a long time. There was some water which also offered a meat course. Dan drank sparingly of it.

"Understand this yap-yap they speak?" said Dan.

"A little."

"What they yelling about now?"

"Something about the *Bain*. Cheering him most likely."

Dan yawned. His relaxation was not at all affected. He had tried to do his job and now he knew his number was up, and what the hell was the use of worrying about something which was cut and dried?

From time to time deputations of warriors stuck their heads into the doorway and stared at Dan and then, clacking excitedly, went away.

In the late afternoon another outfit arrived and these were dressed in all manner of feathers and armlets. They did not stop at staring. They came into the hut and motioned for Dan to get up.

"My party comes first, I guess," said Dan.

"Sorry. So long."

"So long," said Dan as he was led away.

He expected to be taken to the *Bain*'s hut, but he was not. He was ringed around with spears and made to stand in the open square, a place which had been pounded hard by dancing feet.

Nothing happened for a long time and then, at a murmur from the crowd, a shriveled-up old gentleman came out of the *Bain*'s house. He had enough cunning in his sly face to be a charred reproduction of Uriah Heep and enough dignity to be classed with the most stern of judges.

Clothed principally in his grimace, he came to a sidewise stop before Dan and looked him over after the fashion of a squire about to purchase a horse.

In Madi, the ancient one drooled, "You plenty good fighter?"

"No," said Dan.

The old one looked wiser than ever. "I think you are wrong. People see face of Great Devil this morning. Very bad, what you say about him getting weak and sick, huh? You think that right? You think he sick and weak?"

"Yes, sure I do. He's practically out on his feet, he's so weak."

The old one chuckled and went a few steps away. Then he looked back and said, "You still think *Bain* weak?"

"Yes. I know it."

"Then you get chance to find out pretty quick."

This left Dan rather dazed. He poked around mentally and strove to figure it all out. He had had a hunch something like this might happen and now, with a hard-to-suppress grin, he knew he had the rainmaker on the spot.

79

The Dinka custom of making the strongest man king is not unusual. But the fact that they connect the strength of their *Bain* directly with the fertility of their crops and cattle is.

Dan had heard that a Dinka *Bain* was never allowed to get out and do battle with his army. He knew that death was meted out to any *Bain* who failed in strength. But until now he had not understood how these people tested the strength of their overlord. The wild hope at which he had grabbed the night before was now an actuality.

Although this would do no more than prolong his eventual and early demise, it was more interesting than simply getting a dozen spears through him all at once.

The population was gathering in the square, sitting on their collective heels and jabbering in expectation of a show. It could be seen that there were two factions there and Dan leaped to the conclusion that the old native fellow to whom he had spoken had a grudge against the present *Bain*.

Dan told himself he would knock this *Bain* kicking with a hard left and then try to make a run for it.

The *Bain* came out, presently, surrounded by his retinue and plural wives, and serenely looked the situation over. He was wearing his big, wooden devil mask and his cloak of lion skins and he looked very regal. As nearly as Dan could judge, the *Bain* was better than six feet tall and weighed well over two hundred and twenty-five pounds. This mountain of a man looked bigger and more horrible because of the additional height imparted by the wooden mask.

Dan experienced a feeling of deflation. The *Bain* was advancing straight across the square toward the scrap and the

*Bain* was not going to remove his wooden devil mask for the fray.

To hammer mortal fists against that armored head would be, Dan knew, very, very useless.

The *Bain* did not hesitate. He made a signal with his hand and the people gave him room. He dropped his cloak to display a green and red painted body of very muscular build. The devil mask stayed on his shoulders, grinning horribly.

The natives were suddenly still. The *Bain* squared off in front of Dan. Dan flexed his right arm in preparation for a blow.

The *Bain* suddenly lowered his head and charged.

Not expecting this, Dan leaped to one side. The ramlike mask struck his arm and turned him.

But, for an instant, the *Bain*'s head was down and he was slightly off balance.

Dan dived in and snatched at the mask. He gave it a terrific twist as though it rested on screw threads. He shoved hard and sent the *Bain* reeling.

With another dive, Dan skidded through the dust and into the Great Devil. He seized the mask a second time and turned it so that the face pointed to the rear.

With three ramming, pile-driving, shattering impacts, Dan sent his fists into the Great Devil's exposed solar plexus.

With a shudder the *Bain* flopped back, his arms spreading out flat in the dirt. Dan, making sure that this was the end, lifted him and gave him another punch in the stomach. Wind eased noisily out of the *Bain*.

The Dinkas were too stunned to move or speak.

Dan looked quickly around him. But he knew he could

not break through this ring of spears. They would move if he did. Seeing the futility of escape, he bent over and yanked the devil mask from the rainmaker's head.

Dan let out an exclamation of amazement. He was looking into the expressionless and unconscious face of a white man. It was Gotch-ear!

That was too much for Dan. Holding the devil mask aloft as a weapon, he again sought a way out of the ring.

The Dinkas recovered from their surprise at the outcome of the swift battle. The warriors lowered their iron spears and started toward Dan from every side.

Dan glanced up at the sky as though to find aid there. The sun was just going down. Africa was bathed in scarlet light which sent long shadows of purple streaming away from the oncoming natives.

With a quick movement he placed the devil mask before him and started to move ahead, knowing that it was suicide.

The whiplash crack of a Mauser elephant rifle shattered the echoes of Kurfung.

An ululating yell rose high above the babble of the natives.

The roar and crash of a volley cut through the startled ranks of the Dinkas.

The attack was from behind. The gate was not defended and came ripping down. Huddled, without organization or orders, not knowing what or how or why, the warriors thought about cover first and defense later.

But they were blocked.

Into the compound raced Dan's *askaris*!

In their lead, with a Mauser in one hand and a Webley in

the other, hatless and with her damp curls rippling in the hot wind, was Barbara.

Ashamed to seem less brave than a woman, the thirty *askaris* sprinted all around her.

Dinkas were flushed up like coveys of quail and shot on the wing as they tried to escape the ferocity of the charge.

The bedlam reached its height, dipped off and sharply subsided.

The ground was strewn with dead Dinkas and discarded spears. Fleeing for their lives, without a *Bain* to lead them, without half a dozen spears to a hundred warriors, the Dinkas abandoned the stronghold of Kurfung, solid in the belief that a blond-headed genie breathing flame and disaster still followed to gobble them up one by one.

But the genie, blond curls and all, was not breathing flame. She was breathing, "Dan! You romantic fool! You tough, hard-boiled engineer . . ."

She buried her face in his tattered shirt and dropped her Mauser and Webley on the ground.

# Chapter Eleven

TWELVE miles. Ten miles. Eight miles. Six miles. Stakes, stakes, stakes, stretching from Soroti to Sennar.

And then, ahead, visible from a high anthill, Dan sighted the railhead of the Anglo-Egyptian Railway.

One day's work and it was done. A runner had already gone up with a chit addressed to Colonel Malone, who would now be in Sennar.

But there was little elation on Dan Courtney's face when he turned to walk back to his camp. This was not only the end of the survey, it was the end of a pleasant trail.

He stopped outside his tent and Barbara saw him and came near. Her father laid aside a rifle he had been cleaning and called out a hello.

"What's the matter?" said Barbara, looking up into Dan's sober face.

"Why . . . nothing. Nothing's the matter. . . . I mean, everything's the matter. I just spotted Sennar ahead."

"Why, that's fine," said Barbara.

"No, that isn't fine," replied Dan, bitterly. "I can give you these porters and you can make Eritrea. I won't say anything about it."

"Make for Eritrea?" said the old man. "Why should we do that when Sennar is just ahead?"

Dan fished in his pocket and pulled out the pocketbook he had taken from the man known as Bart. He opened it up and showed them the badge.

"I've known about it for a long time," said Dan. "We've avoided the subject, but . . . well . . . The man that was following you, Barbara, was carrying this. He was an IDB cop. But you must have known that. I know you probably were on the watch for some diamonds . . . well, it's awful hard to talk about it. I killed that fellow and buried him two hundred and fifty miles back. This guy Gotch-ear that we've been towing along with us under guard will probably know all about that. You better start packing. Malone will be here in a few hours. . . ."

"An IDB badge," said the old man, looking it over. "Interesting. The name on here is Sherman. By the way, Courtney, have you noticed this belt I carry under my shirt?"

"Yes."

The old man took it off and opened the flaps and poured out a glitter of rough diamonds. "I picked it up in the *Bain's* house at Kurfung, you know. Must be a hundred thousand dollars' worth here."

"Take it along," said Dan. "I won't say anything."

"This Gotch-ear was engaged in trafficking rough diamonds from the Congo, you know," said the old man. "He took over that Dinka village several years ago and set himself up as *Bain*. He ran these things through from the Congo and the railroad would have ruined the trail for him, making the place too frequented."

"I'm giving you plenty of time," said Dan. "I won't give you away."

"You mean," said Barbara, "that you won't inform the IDB? But that's criminal not to, Dan. You might get into trouble."

"I'm an engineer, not a cop. I don't give a damn about the IDB."

"Oh, you don't," said the old man. "Courtney, if you didn't have your head full of mileage figures, you would long ago have found out a very interesting fact."

"What's that?" said Dan.

"Listen, you hard-boiled engineer," said Barbara, her eyes very merry. "That man right there, aside from being my father, is Captain Brice Sherman of the IDB."

"For God's sake!" said Dan. "I . . . I thought . . ."

"I brought my daughter on this one, not thinking it would be rough," said the old man. "It was. Plenty. But never mind, I've done the job—with honors going to a certain engineer."

Dan's eyes began to sparkle. He grinned and took Barbara by the shoulders.

"Listen, it's only about five miles to Sennar," cried Dan. "The survey is through. I've got money in the bank. The bonds for the SR will be good and I'll help build the road. Would . . . er . . . if I . . . that is . . ."

"Yes," said Barbara.

# Story Preview

# Story Preview

NOW that you've just ventured through one of the captivating tales in the Stories from the Golden Age collection by L. Ron Hubbard, turn the page and enjoy a preview of *The Headhunters*. Join Tom Christian on a perilous jungle journey for gold that's already cost the life of his partner. Waiting for him deep in the Solomon Islands is the man responsible for his partner's murder, who wants to trap Christian and grab the treasure for himself.

# The Headhunters

DOWN in the hold of the *King Solomon*, a Polynesian sailor was piling up crates of canned food and humming a little under his breath.

It was cool in the hold, but not so outside in the pounding glare of the equatorial sun which, even this late in the afternoon, was scorching Kieta, Solomon Islands.

A footstep sounded behind the naked sailor and he turned, a grin on his face. Slowly the grin faded, to be replaced by a scowl.

Standing easily in the gloom was a dirty-faced white man of chunky build. In his hand he held a snub nosed .45.

"If it an't Hihi," said the white man. "'Oo would have thought to meet you here?"

"You more better get out," snapped Hihi, straightening up. "If boss comes, he killum plenty along you."

The white man grinned. "'E won't be along, Hihi. I left him passing the time o' day at the club."

Hihi looked uneasily up at the bright square of blue sky which filled the hatch opening. He realized that he was alone aboard the schooner and that this man would show very little mercy if he took it into his head to shoot.

The white man, Punjo Charlie, looked amiable enough except for one eye which jiggled up and down and slid back and forth as though well greased. The other eye, being made of glass, stared steadily ahead. *Punjo* stood for "tough one" in the dialect.

"No," said Punjo Charlie, "'e won't be down for a bit. And I think mybe you'd be so good as to tell me right quick something I want to know about Tom Christian."

Hihi made a stealthy move toward the keen dirk in his belt, but Punjo Charlie raised the gun ever so little and grinned a little harder.

"You went upcountry with Christian, Hihi. 'E found hisself too much gold for one man, him and Larsen. Mybe you'd like to tell me where it was, Hihi. Or mybe you're tired of life. Remember what happened to Larsen, Hihi?"

Hihi looked levelly at the white man, not a little contempt in his brown, handsome face. "Yes, I was with boss, but you no get nothing along me. More better you go before boss knock hell outa you."

"Now see here, Hihi," said Punjo Charlie in a whining drone, "you're mighty fond of life, an't you? I wouldn't want nothink to 'appen to you."

Punjo Charlie stepped slowly forward. Hihi backed up until he was against the damp ribs of the schooner's hold.

Punjo Charlie came on. Hihi suddenly gripped his knife hilt and sprang forward and sideways, weapon upraised, ready to strike.

Punjo looked fat and greasy but he could move like a striking snake. He did not fire, for that would bring down the town upon him. He raised his weapon, caught Hihi's knife and brought the .45 butt crashing down on Hihi's curly hair.

The brown man folded up and sank back, his eyes rolling, a seep of blood coming down his face. Punjo Charlie, with a glance at the hatch overhead, picked up several strands of hemp and lashed Hihi's arms and legs together in such a way that Hihi could not move.

The loyal Polynesian showed no immediate signs of waking up and Punjo Charlie had to resort to a full fire bucket which stood to one side. He sent the contents cascading down over Hihi and stood back, his good eye jiggling from the inert brown man to the hatch.

Hihi came awake slowly and then, with an attempt to leap up, felt the force of his ropes and fell violently back, cursing in several languages.

"You wait," cried Hihi. "Boss kill along you plenty, you bet. I not tell you nothing."

"No?" said Punjo Charlie, grinning evilly. "No?"

Punjo took the dirk and felt its edge. Slowly he leaned over the helpless brown man and drew a small pattern of red lines upon the shrinking chest. Hihi clenched his teeth and said nothing.

"Don't bother you none," said Punjo Charlie in disappointment. "Mybe if I was to hack off an ear careful-like you might like to say something about it. After all, Hihi, it an't nothink hard I wants of you. Just tell me where you left that pool full of gold dust and I'll let you stay right where you are. It an't anythink hard to arsk, Hihi."

"I not tell nothing," snapped Hihi.

Punjo Charlie regretfully took hold of Hihi's ear and fondled it. He tested the edge of his knife, assured himself with a glance that Hihi was not going to talk after all and then, raising the blade, prepared to lop off the ear.

But before the knife could descend, heavy footsteps sounded overhead. Hihi started to cry out. Punjo Charlie slapped half a gunnysack into the open mouth, without any regard for Hihi's feelings in the matter. The sack was crawling with copra bugs.

Overhead, a clear, strong voice said, "Hihi! Where are you, you lazy devil?"

Punjo Charlie moved slowly back behind the stacks of crates until he could no longer be seen in the gloom. The footsteps came close to the hatch and Punjo Charlie raised his .45.

"Hihi!"

Punjo Charlie licked his puffy, greasy lips. That was Tom Christian's voice. Punjo had a score to settle with Tom Christian.

A white-clad man in a sailor cap thrust his shoulders and head over the coaming and yelled, "Hihi! You down there?"

Christian swung himself over the edge and clattered down the ladder. He was a little better than six feet tall and his shoulders were wide and straight. His gray eyes were clear and he had the air about him of a man who knows exactly what he wants to do and exactly how he will do it.

Christian reached the bottom and, stooping his head a little to pass under the crossbeams, looked down the length of the gloomy hold.

"Hihi!"

A slight movement in the darkness caused Christian to turn his head. His sun-dazzled eyes were long in picking up the silhouette of brown on the packs.

"What the devil. . . ."

Christian strode over and yanked the gunny sacking out of Hihi's mouth and started in on the strands of rope.

"Boss," whispered Hihi, "Punjo Charlie . . ."

"If you don't mind, Christian," said Punjo in his whiny voice, looking down the sights of his .45, "if you don't mind, just stand there a bit, old fellow. I wouldn't move none if I was you, Christian."

Christian turned slowly and stared at the dirty, blue-jowled face and the jiggly eye. "You!"

"Ra't you are, Christian. Me, Punjo. Owh, I've been looking forward to this, I can tell you. And how are you feeling, Christian?"

"So you've been looking forward to it, have you?" said Christian, acidly. "Well, so have I. I've been looking for you all over the Solomons. I believe I've got something to say to you, Punjo. Something about my partner, Larsen. Of course you wouldn't know anything about his being murdered, would you?"

"Of course not, Christian."

"Oh, of course not," said Christian, bitterly. "Of course not. You caught Larsen when he went back to clean out that pool and you murdered him."

"Why, Christian," reproved Punjo Charlie. "'Ow could you think of such a thing?"

"I can think it all right. But you made a mistake, didn't you? You killed him before he could lead you to the place we had placered out. And now you're here, are you? It'll be a long time, me bucko, before you spend any of that gold."

"Do tell," said Punjo. "Now an't that too bad. Beg pardon, Christian, but would you mind sitting down there on those crates for just a moment? Long enough for me to put some rope on you? Hi don't want to kill you, Christian. Mybe maim you a little bit, but not kill you. Dead men," he added with a chuckle, "wasn't never known to talk very much."

"Take my advice," said Christian, "and clear out while you're still in one piece. I might change my mind and knock hell out of you."

"Listen to the brave lad," crowed Punjo. His good eye glittered and grew hard and he bared his teeth and his voice dropped down into a snarl. "So help me, Christian, you've stolen that mine off me and I'm going to get you for that. I've got contacts upcountry, Christian. I know Togu and his Kris and you can't arsk for a better lot of murderers than them. You tell me now and I'll let you go. Mybe I'll even split up with you when I get back. But if you think you can get it, Christian, you're a fool. Set one foot upcountry and I'll kill you."

To find out more about *The Headhunters* and how you can obtain your copy, go to www.goldenagestories.com.

# Glossary

# Glossary

STORIES FROM THE GOLDEN AGE *reflect the words and expressions used in the 1930s and 1940s, adding unique flavor and authenticity to the tales. While a character's speech may often reflect regional origins, it also can convey attitudes common in the day. So that readers can better grasp such cultural and historical terms, uncommon words or expressions of the era, the following glossary has been provided.*

---

**Alexandria:** the second largest city in Egypt and its largest seaport, extending about twenty miles along the coast of the Mediterranean Sea in north central Egypt.

**Anglo-Egyptian:** Anglo-Egyptian Sudan was the name of Sudan between 1899 and 1956, when it was jointly ruled by the United Kingdom and Egypt (which was then under British influence).

*askaris:* (Swahili) soldiers. During the period of European rule in East Africa, locally recruited *askaris* were employed by the British, Italian, Portuguese, German and Belgian colonial forces. They played a crucial role in the initial conquest of the various colonial possessions and subsequently served as garrison and internal security forces.

**Bagandas:** members of the largest ethnic group in Uganda. Their traditional homeland is Buganda, a former kingdom in the area north of Lake Victoria in southern Uganda, which became part of Uganda in 1962.

*Bain:* a human rainmaker and very important personage among the Dinka. A *Bain* is believed to be animated by the spirit of a great rainmaker who has come down to him through a succession of rainmakers. A successful rainmaker enjoys very great power and is consulted on all important matters. No Dinka rainmaker is allowed to die a natural death of sickness or old age as they believe that to do so, the tribe would suffer from disease and famine, and the herds would not yield their increase. Instead, when a rainmaker feels he is growing old and infirm, he tells his children he wishes to die. A large grave is dug in which he lies, surrounded by friends and relatives. For many hours, generally for more than a day, without food or water, he instructs those around him on how they are to act in the future. When he is done, he bids them to cover him up, upon which he soon dies of suffocation.

**Banquo:** in Shakespeare's *Macbeth,* Banquo and Macbeth, generals in the Scottish army, hear prophecies from three witches that Macbeth will be named baron of Cawdor and that Banquo's children will inherit the Scottish throne. Macbeth kills Duncan, the King of Scotland, thereby ascending the throne. He then has Banquo killed by his assassins to keep the prophecy from coming true. During a banquet, Macbeth is informed of the death of Banquo and of his son's escape. The festivity is interrupted by Banquo's ghost, invisible to the guests, which appears threateningly before Macbeth, haunting him.

**Bantu:** language of the Bantu people; a general term for over four hundred ethnic groups in Africa, from Cameroon to South Africa, united by a common language family and in many cases common customs.

**blackwater fever:** a serious, often fatal complication of chronic malaria, characterized by the passage of bloody, dark red or black urine.

**Blue Nile:** a tributary of the Nile; a river in East Africa, flowing north-northwest from Lake Tana in Ethiopia into the Nile at Khartoum.

**braggadocio:** used to describe a boasting person or braggart.

*bwana:* (Swahili) mister; sir; used as a title or respectful form of address.

**chaining:** measuring by use of a "Gunter's chain," an instrument that is made of links and is used in measuring land. It consists of 100 links, each link being 7.92 inches in length, with the total length of 66 feet or 1/10th of an acre.

**coaming:** a raised rim or border around an opening in a ship's deck, designed to keep out water.

**copra bugs:** beetles that cause damage to copra, the dried white flesh of the coconut from which coconut oil is extracted. They are metallic blue in color, but sometimes have a greenish luster. They are 1/12th of an inch long (3.5 to 5.5 mm).

**Dark Continent:** a former name for Africa, so used because its remote backcountry was largely unknown and therefore mysterious to Europeans until the nineteenth century. Henry M. Stanley was probably the first to use the term in his 1878 account *Through the Dark Continent.*

$\dfrac{df}{dy}$ : a type of mathematical equation used in engineering and physics describing how something continuously changes in relation to another variable. Used humorously.

*dhotīs:* (Hindu) a long loincloth; a simple wrap around the waist that resembles a long skirt. It is folded in half up to the knees while working. It is worn in East Africa as well as in India.

**Dinka:** cattle-herding people of the Nile basin in southern Sudan. The men are warriors and guardians of the camp against predators: lions, hyenas and other enemy raiders.

**EEA:** Equatorial East Africa; the region of eastern Africa near the equator, primarily including Kenya and northern Tanzania.

**eland:** a large spiral-horned African antelope.

**Eritrea:** the northernmost province of Ethiopia, bordered by Sudan on the north and west, and the Red Sea on the north and east.

**G-men:** government men; agents of the Federal Bureau of Investigation.

**half-caste:** a person of mixed racial descent.

**IDB:** Illicit Diamond Buyer or Buying; a special police force that took in hand all crimes involving diamonds.

**Italian Somaliland:** an Italian colony that lasted, apart from a brief interlude of British rule, from the late nineteenth century until 1960 in the territory of the modern-day East African nation of Somalia.

**Khartoum:** the capital of Sudan and of Khartoum State. It is located at the point where the White Nile, flowing north from Uganda, meets the Blue Nile, flowing west from Ethiopia. The merger of the two Niles is known as "the Mogran." The merged Nile flows north towards Egypt and the Mediterranean Sea.

**Kieta:** the principal harbor on the island of Bougainville, the northernmost and largest of the Solomon Islands.

**Kimberley:** the capital of the Northern Cape, a large, sparsely populated province in South Africa. Kimberley is synonymous worldwide with diamonds. In 1871, diamonds were found on a small hill that became known as Colesberg Kopple (later Kimberley). It was here that the famous *Star of Africa* was found, a 530.20-carat diamond, and other giant sparklers far too big for a ring.

*kwenda:* (Swahili) move; proceed.

**Lady Achilles to sulk in my netting:** in reference to the Trojan War, where the great warrior Achilles sulked in his tent after an argument, refusing to fight.

**Lake Salisbury:** a lake in Uganda that provides a conduit for the waters north of Mount Elgon (the fourth highest mountain in East Africa, located in the eastern part of Uganda on the border with Kenya) that run into the Nile system.

**Lake Tanganyika:** a lake in central Africa. It is the longest freshwater lake in the world.

**Madi:** a central Sudanic language of the Madi people, an ethnic group living mainly in parts of Sudan and Uganda.

**Masai:** the language of a people living in Tanzania and Kenya.

**Mauser:** a bolt-action rifle made by Mauser, a German arms manufacturer. These rifles have been made since the 1870s.

*memsahib:* (Swahili) respectful greeting to one's female employer or upper-class rich woman.

*mnyapara:* (Swahili) headman, especially of a caravan or an expedition.

**Mogadishu:** the largest city in Somalia, and its capital. Mogadishu lies on the Indian Ocean coast, and the city has served as an important regional port for centuries.

**Mombasa:** the second largest city in Kenya, lying on the Indian Ocean. In 1894 the British government declared a protectorate over Kenya, calling it the East African Protectorate. In 1901 the first railway line was completed from Mombasa to Kisumu, a city in the southwestern part of Kenya.

**Mount Alak:** former name of a mountain located in south central Sudan. It is part of the Dongotona mountain range bordering Uganda.

*mpishi:* (Swahili) cook.

**Nairobi:** the capital and largest city of Kenya in the south central part of the country. Founded in 1899, it became the seat of government for British East Africa in 1905 and capital of independent Kenya in 1963.

*ndiyo:* (Swahili) yes.

**Nilote:** a native and inhabitant of the banks of the Upper Nile; a member of any of several peoples from East Africa and Sudan.

*panga:* (Swahili) machete; a cleaverlike tool that looks like a very large knife. The blade is typically eighteen to twenty-four inches long. The *panga* has a broad blade and a squared-off tip.

**parietal:** either of two large bones that together form the sides and top of the skull.

**placer:** to obtain minerals from placers (deposits of river sand or gravel containing particles of gold or another valuable metal) by washing or dredging.

*posho:* (Swahili) maize flour or ground maize, a staple starch component of many African meals, especially in southern and East Africa.

**Punch:** the chief male character of the Punch and Judy puppet show, a famous English comedy dating back to the seventeenth century, by way of France from Italy. It is performed using hand puppets in a tent-style puppet theater with a cloth backdrop and board in front. The puppeteer introduces the puppets from beneath the board so that they are essentially popping up to the stage area of the theater.

**recorder:** a survey party's noteman; the member of a survey team whose job it is to assist surveyors in measuring angles, distances and elevations, and to record the measurements.

**Robinson Crusoe:** the protagonist and narrator in the novel *The Life and Strange Adventures of Robinson Crusoe,* by English novelist Daniel Defoe (1660?–1731). The novel follows Robinson Crusoe's survival and perseverance through storms, enslavement and a twenty-eight-year isolation on a desert island.

**rodman:** in surveying, a person who carries the leveling rod, a light pole marked with gradations, held upright and read through a surveying instrument.

**RS:** Reuters Service, the world news and information organization; in October 1851, Paul Julius Reuter (1816–1899), a German-born immigrant, opened an office in the city of London that transmitted stock market quotations between London and Paris. Reuters, as the agency soon became known, eventually extended its service to the whole British press as well as to other European countries. It also expanded the content to include general and economic news from all around the world.

*sahib:* (Swahili) master.

**Saint Vitus' dance:** a nervous disorder characterized by rapid, jerky, involuntary movements of the body.

**Scheherazade:** the female narrator of *The Arabian Nights,* who during one thousand and one adventurous nights saved her life by entertaining her husband, the king, with stories.

**schooner:** a fast sailing ship with at least two masts and with sails set lengthwise.

**Sennar:** a state in Sudan; a town on the Blue Nile and the capital of the state of Sennar.

**shots:** estimations of distance or altitude by the use of a surveying instrument.

**Sobat River:** a river of northeastern Africa, the most southerly of the great eastern tributaries of the Nile.

**Solomon Islands:** a group of islands northeast of Australia. They form a double chain of six large islands, about twenty medium-sized ones and numerous smaller islets and reefs.

**Soroti:** the main commercial and administrative center of the Soroti District in eastern Uganda, a country in East Africa bordered on the east by Kenya and the north by Sudan.

**spider webbing:** cross hairs; either of two fine strands of wire crossed in the focus of the eyepiece of an optical instrument for surveying and used as a sighting reference. During World War I, the threads of some spiders were used as cross hairs in instruments.

**SR:** Sudan Railway.

**Stanley:** Sir Henry Morton Stanley (1841–1904), journalist and explorer of Africa. He was among the most accomplished and noted European explorers of Africa and his work played an important part in bringing about the European colonization of African territory in the late nineteenth and early twentieth centuries. He is best known for locating Scottish missionary-explorer David Livingstone, who had been reported missing in East Africa in 1870. Upon finding him in 1871, Stanley greeted him with the famous words: "Dr. Livingstone, I presume?"

**stripe:** 1. to strike; to lash. 2. a stroke or blow, as with a whip.

**Sudan Railway:** railway system in Sudan, linking most of the major towns and cities. Sudan is bordered by Egypt to the north, the Red Sea to the northeast, Ethiopia to the east and Kenya and Uganda to the southwest. The first line was built in the 1870s and was a commercial undertaking. It was extended in the mid-1880s and again in the mid-1890s to support the Anglo-Egyptian military campaigns.

**sudd:** the name given to the vegetation obstruction that has, at various dates, closed the waters of part of the Nile to navigation. The abundant vegetation that grows along the banks is loosed by storms into the river where it drifts until it lodges on some obstruction and forms a dam across the channel and into blocks that are sometimes twenty-five miles long and fifteen to twenty feet below the surface. These masses of decayed vegetation and earth, resembling peat in consistency, are so much compressed by the force of the current that men can walk over them everywhere. In parts, elephants could cross without danger.

**Tanganyika:** a former country of east-central Africa. A British territory after 1920, it became independent in 1961 and joined with Zanzibar to form Tanzania in 1964.

**ten-seventy-five by sixty-eight:** a Mauser rifle with 10.75 x 68 mm cartridges. They were used to shoot elephants for their ivory tusks.

**.300 Scott rifle:** a sporting rifle that uses .300-caliber ammunition. With the caliber of bullet used being so high, the muzzle blast is extremely loud and bystanders can sometimes feel the shock wave.

**transit:** a surveying instrument surmounted by a telescope that can be rotated completely around its horizontal axis, used for measuring vertical and horizontal angles.

**Tsavo:** a region of Kenya located at the crossing of the Uganda Railway over the Tsavo River. It is the largest national park in Kenya and one of the largest in the world. Because of its size the park was split into two, Tsavo West and Tsavo East, for easy administration. Tsavo achieved fame in *The Man-eaters of Tsavo,* a book about lions who attacked workers building the railroad bridge.

**Tuaregs:** members of the nomadic Berber-speaking people of the southwestern Sahara in Africa. They have traditionally engaged in herding, agriculture and convoying caravans across their territories. The Tuaregs became among the most hostile of all the colonized peoples of French West

Africa, because they were among the most affected by colonial policies. In 1917, they fought a vicious and bloody war against the French, but they were defeated and as a result, dispossessed of traditional grazing lands. They are known to be fierce warriors; European explorers expressed their fear by warning, "The scorpion and the Tuareg are the only enemies you meet in the desert."

**Uganda Railway:** a historical railway system linking the interiors of Uganda and Kenya to the Indian Ocean at Mombasa in Kenya. The line started at the port city of Mombasa in 1896 and reached Kisuma in 1901 on the eastern shore of Lake Victoria. Despite being called "the Lunatic Line" by its detractors, the railway was a huge logistical achievement and became strategically and economically vital for both Uganda and Kenya.

**Uriah Heep:** the hypocritical and devious clerk in Dickens' novel *David Copperfield*. With eyes of red brown, he was high-shouldered, bony, and had a long, lank skeleton.

**Webley:** Webley and Scott handgun; an arms manufacturer based in England that produced handguns from 1834. Webley is famous for the revolvers and automatic pistols it supplied to the British Empire's military, particularly the British Army, from 1887 through both World War I and World War II.

**White Nile:** the part of the Nile that flows northeast to Sudan and is approximately 500 miles (804 km) long.

**Yank:** Yankee; term used to refer to Americans in general.

# L. Ron Hubbard
# in the Golden Age
# of Pulp Fiction

*In writing an adventure story
a writer has to know that he is adventuring
for a lot of people who cannot.
The writer has to take them here and there
about the globe and show them
excitement and love and realism.
As long as that writer is living the part of an
adventurer when he is hammering
the keys, he is succeeding with his story.*

*Adventuring is a state of mind.
If you adventure through life, you have a
good chance to be a success on paper.*

*Adventure doesn't mean globe-trotting,
exactly, and it doesn't mean great deeds.
Adventuring is like art.
You have to live it to make it real.*

## —L. RON HUBBARD

# L. Ron Hubbard
# and American
# Pulp Fiction

B ORN March 13, 1911, L. Ron Hubbard lived a life at least as expansive as the stories with which he enthralled a hundred million readers through a fifty-year career.

Originally hailing from Tilden, Nebraska, he spent his formative years in a classically rugged Montana, replete with the cowpunchers, lawmen and desperadoes who would later people his Wild West adventures. And lest anyone imagine those adventures were drawn from vicarious experience, he was not only breaking broncs at a tender age, he was also among the few whites ever admitted into Blackfoot society as a bona fide blood brother. While if only to round out an otherwise rough and tumble youth, his mother was that rarity of her time—a thoroughly educated woman—who introduced her son to the classics of Occidental literature even before his seventh birthday.

But as any dedicated L. Ron Hubbard reader will attest, his world extended far beyond Montana. In point of fact, and as the son of a United States naval officer, by the age of eighteen he had traveled over a quarter of a million miles. Included therein were three Pacific crossings to a then still mysterious Asia, where he ran with the likes of Her British Majesty's agent-in-place

*L. Ron Hubbard, left, at Congressional Airport, Washington, DC, 1931, with members of George Washington University flying club.*

for North China, and the last in the line of Royal Magicians from the court of Kublai Khan. For the record, L. Ron Hubbard was also among the first Westerners to gain admittance to forbidden Tibetan monasteries below Manchuria, and his photographs of China's Great Wall long graced American geography texts.

Upon his return to the United States and a hasty completion of his interrupted high school education, the young Ron Hubbard entered George Washington University. There, as fans of his aerial adventures may have heard, he earned his wings as a pioneering barnstormer at the dawn of American aviation. He also earned a place in free-flight record books for the longest sustained flight above Chicago. Moreover, as a roving reporter for *Sportsman Pilot* (featuring his first professionally penned articles), he further helped inspire a generation of pilots who would take America to world airpower.

Immediately beyond his sophomore year, Ron embarked on the first of his famed ethnological expeditions, initially to then untrammeled Caribbean shores (descriptions of which would later fill a whole series of West Indies mystery-thrillers). That the Puerto Rican interior would also figure into the future of Ron Hubbard stories was likewise no accident. For in addition to cultural studies of the island, a 1932–33

116

LRH expedition is rightly remembered as conducting the first complete mineralogical survey of a Puerto Rico under United States jurisdiction.

There was many another adventure along this vein: As a lifetime member of the famed Explorers Club, L. Ron Hubbard charted North Pacific waters with the first shipboard radio direction finder, and so pioneered a long-range navigation system universally employed until the late twentieth century. While not to put too fine an edge on it, he also held a rare Master Mariner's license to pilot any vessel, of any tonnage in any ocean.

Yet lest we stray too far afield, there is an LRH note at this juncture in his saga, and it reads in part:

*"I started out writing for the pulps, writing the best I knew, writing for every mag on the stands, slanting as well as I could."*

To which one might add: His earliest submissions date from the summer of 1934, and included tales drawn from true-to-life Asian adventures, with characters roughly modeled on British/American intelligence operatives he had known in Shanghai. His early Westerns were similarly peppered with details drawn from personal experience. Although therein lay a first hard lesson from the often cruel world of the pulps. His first Westerns were soundly rejected as lacking the authenticity of a Max Brand yarn

*Capt. L. Ron Hubbard in Ketchikan, Alaska, 1940, on his Alaskan Radio Experimental Expedition, the first of three voyages conducted under the Explorers Club flag.*

(a particularly frustrating comment given L. Ron Hubbard's Westerns came straight from his Montana homeland, while Max Brand was a mediocre New York poet named Frederick Schiller Faust, who turned out implausible six-shooter tales from the terrace of an Italian villa).

Nevertheless, and needless to say, L. Ron Hubbard persevered and soon earned a reputation as among the most publishable names in pulp fiction, with a ninety percent placement rate of first-draft manuscripts. He was also among the most prolific, averaging between seventy and a hundred thousand words a month. Hence the rumors that L. Ron Hubbard had redesigned a typewriter for faster keyboard action and pounded out manuscripts on a continuous roll of butcher paper to save the precious seconds it took to insert a single sheet of paper into manual typewriters of the day.

That all L. Ron Hubbard stories did not run beneath said byline is yet another aspect of pulp fiction lore. That is, as publishers periodically rejected manuscripts from top-drawer authors if only to avoid paying top dollar, L. Ron Hubbard and company just as frequently replied with submissions under various pseudonyms. In Ron's case, the

## A Man of Many Names

*Between 1934 and 1950, L. Ron Hubbard authored more than fifteen million words of fiction in more than two hundred classic publications. To supply his fans and editors with stories across an array of genres and pulp titles, he adopted fifteen pseudonyms in addition to his already renowned L. Ron Hubbard byline.*

*Winchester Remington Colt*
*Lt. Jonathan Daly*
*Capt. Charles Gordon*
*Capt. L. Ron Hubbard*
*Bernard Hubbel*
*Michael Keith*
*Rene Lafayette*
*Legionnaire 148*
*Legionnaire 14830*
*Ken Martin*
*Scott Morgan*
*Lt. Scott Morgan*
*Kurt von Rachen*
*Barry Randolph*
*Capt. Humbert Reynolds*

list included: Rene Lafayette, Captain Charles Gordon, Lt. Scott Morgan and the notorious Kurt von Rachen—supposedly on the lam for a murder rap, while hammering out two-fisted prose in Argentina. The point: While L. Ron Hubbard as Ken Martin spun stories of Southeast Asian intrigue, LRH as Barry Randolph authored tales of

*L. Ron Hubbard, circa 1930, at the outset of a literary career that would finally span half a century.*

romance on the Western range—which, stretching between a dozen genres is how he came to stand among the two hundred elite authors providing close to a million tales through the glory days of American Pulp Fiction.

In evidence of exactly that, by 1936 L. Ron Hubbard was literally leading pulp fiction's elite as president of New York's American Fiction Guild. Members included a veritable pulp hall of fame: Lester "Doc Savage" Dent, Walter "The Shadow" Gibson, and the legendary Dashiell Hammett—to cite but a few.

Also in evidence of just where L. Ron Hubbard stood within his first two years on the American pulp circuit: By the spring of 1937, he was ensconced in Hollywood, adopting a Caribbean thriller for Columbia Pictures, remembered today as *The Secret of Treasure Island*. Comprising fifteen thirty-minute episodes, the L. Ron Hubbard screenplay led to the most profitable matinée serial in Hollywood history. In accord with Hollywood culture, he was thereafter continually called upon

*The 1937* Secret of Treasure Island, *a fifteen-episode serial adapted for the screen by L. Ron Hubbard from his novel,* Murder at Pirate Castle.

to rewrite/doctor scripts—most famously for long-time friend and fellow adventurer Clark Gable.

In the interim—and herein lies another distinctive chapter of the L. Ron Hubbard story—he continually worked to open Pulp Kingdom gates to up-and-coming authors. Or, for that matter, anyone who wished to write. It was a fairly unconventional stance, as markets were already thin and competition razor sharp. But the fact remains, it was an L. Ron Hubbard hallmark that he vehemently lobbied on behalf of young authors—regularly supplying instructional articles to trade journals, guest-lecturing to short story classes at George Washington University and Harvard, and even founding his own creative writing competition. It was established in 1940, dubbed the Golden Pen, and guaranteed winners both New York representation and publication in *Argosy*.

But it was John W. Campbell Jr.'s *Astounding Science Fiction* that finally proved the most memorable LRH vehicle. While every fan of L. Ron Hubbard's galactic epics undoubtedly knows the story, it nonetheless bears repeating: By late 1938, the pulp publishing magnate of Street & Smith was determined to revamp *Astounding Science Fiction* for broader readership. In particular, senior editorial director F. Orlin Tremaine called for stories with a stronger *human element*. When acting editor John W. Campbell balked, preferring his spaceship-driven

120

tales, Tremaine enlisted Hubbard. Hubbard, in turn, replied with the genre's first truly *character-driven* works, wherein heroes are pitted not against bug-eyed monsters but the mystery and majesty of deep space itself—and thus was launched the Golden Age of Science Fiction.

The names alone are enough to quicken the pulse of any science fiction aficionado, including LRH friend and protégé, Robert Heinlein, Isaac Asimov, A. E. van Vogt and Ray Bradbury. Moreover, when coupled with LRH stories of fantasy, we further come to what's rightly been described as the foundation of every modern tale of horror: L. Ron Hubbard's immortal *Fear.* It was rightly proclaimed by Stephen King as one of the very few works to genuinely warrant that overworked term "classic"—as in: *"This is a classic tale of creeping, surreal menace and horror. . . . This is one of the really, really good ones."*

To accommodate the greater body of L. Ron Hubbard fantasies, Street & Smith inaugurated *Unknown*—a classic pulp if there ever was one, and wherein readers were soon thrilling to the likes of *Typewriter in the Sky* and *Slaves of Sleep* of which Frederik Pohl would declare: *"There are bits and pieces from Ron's work that became part of the language in ways that very few other writers managed."*

*L. Ron Hubbard, 1948, among fellow science fiction luminaries at the World Science Fiction Convention in Toronto.*

And, indeed, at J. W. Campbell Jr.'s insistence, Ron was regularly drawing on themes from the Arabian Nights and

121

so introducing readers to a world of genies, jinn, Aladdin and Sinbad—all of which, of course, continue to float through cultural mythology to this day.

At least as influential in terms of post-apocalypse stories was L. Ron Hubbard's 1940 *Final Blackout*. Generally acclaimed as the finest anti-war novel of the decade and among the ten best works of the genre ever authored—here, too, was a tale that would live on in ways few other writers imagined.

*Portland, Oregon, 1943; L. Ron Hubbard, captain of the US Navy subchaser PC 815.*

Hence, the later Robert Heinlein verdict: "Final Blackout *is as perfect a piece of science fiction as has ever been written.*"

Like many another who both lived and wrote American pulp adventure, the war proved a tragic end to Ron's sojourn in the pulps. He served with distinction in four theaters and was highly decorated for commanding corvettes in the North Pacific. He was also grievously wounded in combat, lost many a close friend and colleague and thus resolved to say farewell to pulp fiction and devote himself to what it had supported these many years—namely, his serious research.

But in no way was the LRH literary saga at an end, for as he wrote some thirty years later, in 1980:

*"Recently there came a period when I had little to do. This was novel in a life so crammed with busy years, and I decided to amuse myself by writing a novel that was pure science fiction."*

That work was *Battlefield Earth: A Saga of the Year 3000*. It was an immediate *New York Times* bestseller and, in fact, the first international science fiction blockbuster in decades. It was not, however, L. Ron Hubbard's magnum opus, as that distinction is generally reserved for his next and final work: The 1.2 million word *Mission Earth*.

> **Final Blackout**
> *is as perfect a piece of science fiction as has ever been written.*
>
> —Robert Heinlein

How he managed those 1.2 million words in just over twelve months is yet another piece of the L. Ron Hubbard legend. But the fact remains, he did indeed author a ten-volume *dekalogy* that lives in publishing history for the fact that each and every volume of the series was also a *New York Times* bestseller.

Moreover, as subsequent generations discovered L. Ron Hubbard through republished works and novelizations of his screenplays, the mere fact of his name on a cover signaled an international bestseller. . . . Until, to date, sales of his works exceed hundreds of millions, and he otherwise remains among the most enduring and widely read authors in literary history. Although as a final word on the tales of L. Ron Hubbard, perhaps it's enough to simply reiterate what editors told readers in the glory days of American Pulp Fiction:

*He writes the way he does, brothers, because he's been there, seen it and done it!*

# THE STORIES FROM THE GOLDEN AGE

Your ticket to adventure starts here with the Stories from the Golden Age collection by master storyteller L. Ron Hubbard. These gripping tales are set in a kaleidoscope of exotic locales and brim with fascinating characters, including some of the most vile villains, dangerous dames and brazen heroes you'll ever get to meet.

The entire collection of over one hundred and fifty stories is being released in a series of eighty books and audiobooks. For an up-to-date listing of available titles, go to www.goldenagestories.com.

## AIR ADVENTURE

## FAR-FLUNG ADVENTURE

## SEA ADVENTURE

## TALES FROM THE ORIENT

## MYSTERY

## FANTASY

## SCIENCE FICTION

## WESTERN

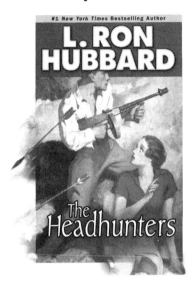

# JOIN THE PULP REVIVAL
## *America in the 1930s and 40s*

Pulp fiction was in its heyday and 30 million readers were regularly riveted by the larger-than-life tales of master storyteller L. Ron Hubbard. For this was pulp fiction's golden age, when the writing was raw and every page packed a walloping punch.

That magic can now be yours. An evocative world of nefarious villains, exotic intrigues, courageous heroes and heroines—a world that today's cinema has barely tapped for tales of adventure and swashbucklers.

Enroll today in the Stories from the Golden Age Club and begin receiving your monthly feature edition selected from more than 150 stories in the collection.

You may choose to enjoy them as either a paperback or audiobook for the special membership price of $9.95 each month along with FREE shipping and handling.